I0768640

Robert Starnes

Some echoes fade. Others Bleed

Silence in Whispering Pines

A Novella

Robert Starnes

Table of Contents

Robert Starnes

Chapter 1

Settling Down

A low mist rolled over Whispering Pines as dawn broke, curling around the rooftops and whispering through the tall evergreens that surrounded the small Texas town. Brenda Wisely stood at her kitchen window, coffee steaming in her hands, watching the world wake up. The air outside smelled of pine and earth, tinged with the faint sweetness of magnolia from the neighbor's yard. It had been a year since she and Dalton packed what was left of their lives into a U-Haul and left Atlanta behind—along with the whispers, the headlines, and the shadow of her late husband's disgrace.

Her husband's name had once meant respect in the Atlanta Police Department. Then came the accusations—corruption, bribes, a scandal that stained every memory she'd had of him. By the time the truth could have cleared him, it was too late. The badge he'd loved was buried with him, and Brenda was left holding the weight of the rumors. *You can't outrun ghosts,* she had told herself back then. But somehow, Whispering Pines had quieted them.

Here, she was no one's widow. Here, she was Detective Wisely—the woman who solved the unsolvable. Within her first few months, she'd cracked a ten-year-old cold case, the homicide of a young man named David "Davie" Youngblood. People in town still mentioned it with quiet awe, as if she'd pulled light out of the fog itself. Whispering Pines was small, the kind of town where everyone knew everyone, and secrets didn't stay buried long. But Brenda had proven that when she came knocking, the truth had nowhere left to hide.

Dalton had flourished too. In Atlanta, the boy had been sullen and distant, the kind of teenager who carried the weight of his father's reputation even when it wasn't his to bear. But here, he laughed again. He had friends, a team, a future. He'd finished his sophomore year at Whispering Pines High stronger than ever—top grades, a circle of good kids, a sense of belonging. Watching him thrive had been worth every sacrifice.

Brenda turned from the window as the first steps creaked down the hallway. Dalton emerged, hair tousled, rubbing sleep from his eyes. He yawned dramatically and gave her a lopsided grin. "You're up early. What's the occasion?"

"Breakfast," she said, plating pancakes with quiet satisfaction. "We're celebrating."

He blinked at her. "Celebrating what?"

She raised an eyebrow. "Someone just wrapped up sophomore year with one of the highest GPAs in his class."

Dalton smirked, sinking into a chair. "You didn't have to go all out, Mom."

"Maybe not," she said, setting a glass of orange juice in front of him, "but you earned it."

The kitchen filled with the scent of maple syrup and sizzling bacon. Outside, the fog was beginning to thin, light filtering through the blinds in narrow golden stripes. Brenda sat across from her son, savoring the simple comfort of the moment. For once, life had settled into something ordinary—something safe. *Maybe this is what peace feels like,* she thought, a faint smile touching her lips.

"Mom," Dalton said, his tone teasing, "you sure this isn't your way of keeping yourself busy? No cases left to solve?"

Brenda chuckled, shaking her head. "Don't jinx me. A slow month is a gift."

The truth was, quiet days were rare in her line of work—but lately, there had been too many of them. Murders were almost unheard of here. Most of her time was spent closing out old files, tracking down long-ignored leads, or convincing confessions from suspects who folded after a single conversation. Detective Wisely had become something of a legend in the county—a mix of intuition, persistence, and disarming calm. But lately, the stillness had begun to gnaw at her. She missed the chase, and the rhythm of unraveling lies. *Careful what you wish for,* she reminded herself, though she didn't yet know how right she was.

Her phone rang. The sharp tone broke the stillness like a sudden crack of thunder. Brenda glanced at Dalton and gave him a small, apologetic smile before answering.

"This is Detective Wisely."

"Detective," came Sophie's voice from dispatch, calm but brisk. "We've got a body behind the twenty-four-hour gas station on Main Street. Are you available?"

Brenda's grip tightened around the phone. *A body? Here?* "10-4," she said, her tone steady. "I'm on my way."

She hung up and turned back to Dalton. He was watching her closely, his expression somewhere between pride and understanding.

"Go," he said softly. "You've been waiting for something like this."

She hesitated for a moment, caught between maternal guilt and professional instinct. "Eat before you go," she said, trying to sound firm.

"Yes, ma'am," he replied with a grin that almost undid her resolve.

Brenda leaned down, pressing a quick kiss to the top of his head before grabbing her keys. As she stepped toward the door, she caught her reflection in the hallway mirror—tired eyes, silver strands catching the light. *Don't get too comfortable,* she thought. *Peace never lasts in a town like this.*

***

The mist still clung to the roads as Brenda's cruiser rolled down Main Street. The gas station's flickering sign cast an eerie glow over the asphalt, and a small group of townsfolk had already gathered near the dumpsters behind the building. Whispering Pines didn't see much crime—certainly not the kind that drew a crowd. Brenda parked, her boots crunching against gravel as she stepped out. The scent of gasoline hung heavy in the air.

Officer Colton stood a few feet away, looking nervous. "Detective," he greeted quickly. "I just got here a few minutes ago. People were already—"

"Then you tell them to move and tape it off," she interrupted, voice calm but firm. "You know the drill."

He nodded and hurried off to comply while Brenda surveyed the scene. The victim lay sprawled in the dirt, his face pale, eyes open to the dawn. A faint red mark circled his neck—a bruise, or perhaps something more deliberate. Brenda crouched down, taking in every detail: the mud on his boots, the torn jacket, the stillness of his hands. Behind her, the murmuring of the crowd carried on like low static. Familiar faces. Curious ones. Some frightened.

"Everyone, back to the front of the store!" she called out. "No one leaves until I've spoken to you."

Her voice cut through the chatter, and slowly, people obeyed. As they shuffled away, Brenda caught the faint tremor in her own breath. *It's been a long time since I've had a fresh one,* she thought. *Too long.*

And just like that, Whispering Pines was no longer quiet.

As Brenda stood over the lifeless body, the flickering fluorescent light cast sharp shadows across the blood-stained tiles. She called Officer Colton over with a calm but commanding tone. When he reached her side, she fixed her eyes on him.

"Officer Colton, when you arrived, did you notice anything around the victim's neck?"

Colton hesitated, his brow furrowing. "Yes, ma'am. There was something—looked like a cord or rope. Why do you ask?"

"Because it's missing now." Brenda's voice hardened. "Did you remove it, or did anyone else come back here while I was at the front interviewing witnesses?"

Colton's eyes darted away. He shifted uneasily before replying, "Detective, I can't answer that. The Sheriff asked me to tell you to speak with him directly."

Brenda froze, caught off guard. "The Sheriff?" she repeated, studying his face. He offered no further explanation.

Choosing not to press him further, Brenda turned and left the store, her mind spinning with questions.

Why would Sheriff Harper involve himself so directly—and why was evidence removed from the scene?

The drive to the Sheriff's Office felt longer than usual. When she arrived, she parked and walked briskly through the front doors, ignoring the dispatcher's greeting. She pushed open the Sheriff's door without knocking.

"Sheriff Harper," she began, her tone sharp, "why did you remove evidence from my crime scene and tell Officer Colton to send me to you? What exactly do you know about this victim?"

Harper looked up from his desk, met her gaze, and then sighed heavily. "Detective Wisely, before you jump to conclusions, you need to understand something. I'm not hiding evidence. I had Officer Colton direct you here because he's unaware of what this case touches."

Brenda crossed her arms. "And what does it touch, Sheriff?"

"You've been reviewing the cold cases of Whispering Pines," Harper continued, his voice low and deliberate. "You're about to discover a connection between this murder and several of those old files. You might want to sit down before I explain."

Reluctantly, Brenda took a seat opposite him. She could sense the gravity in his tone.

"There's one case you haven't seen," Harper began. "Because I removed it from the cold case archives years ago."

Brenda frowned. "You *removed* a case file? Why would you do that? Was it never investigated?"

"It was," he said quietly. "But it involved my son."

Brenda's expression hardened. "Your *son?* Sheriff, if your son was a suspect, you should have recused yourself."

"It wasn't that," Harper said, his voice breaking slightly. "My son was the victim."

Brenda sat back, momentarily speechless. She let the silence linger before softly prompting, "Go on."

"Twenty-eight years ago," Harper began, "my boy was found in a field—barely alive. He was rushed to the hospital and spent years in a coma."

"I'm sorry, Sheriff," Brenda interjected gently.

He nodded in appreciation. "When he finally woke up, he remembered fragments of what happened that night. Just enough to give us a few clues. But before we could act on them…" His voice faltered. "He was murdered. In his hospital bed."

Brenda felt a chill crawl down her spine. "Murdered? Was the killer ever found?"

"No," Harper said. "That's why it's still a cold case—and why I took it out of circulation. I chased every lead, every name, and hit a wall each time."

"Then why bring this up now?" Brenda asked. "What does your son's case have to do with today's murder?"

Harper leaned forward. "When my son was found, he had a rope around his neck—just like your victim."

Brenda narrowed her eyes. "You think that's enough to link the two?"

"Not just that," Harper replied. "There was a playing card found in your victim's pocket. The same kind of card found near my son. I had Colton remove both items to prevent panic before we knew more."

Brenda's voice sharpened. "You withheld evidence, Sheriff. That's obstruction."

Harper didn't flinch. "It's not just about your case or mine, Brenda. There have been eleven victims over the past forty-five years—all marked by the same symbols: the rope and the card. My son was the only one who survived the initial attack. I believe that's why they came back for him. They never meant for him to live. And when he started to remember… they silenced him."

The room fell silent, the weight of his words settling like dust in the air. Brenda exhaled slowly, realizing she'd stumbled into something far larger—and far darker—than she'd imagined.

The hum of the overhead lights buzzed against the silence. Brenda stood over the body, the sharp scent of iron heavy in the air. The floor tiles were slick beneath her shoes, a thin reflection of the figure at her feet.

"Officer Colton," she called softly, yet the weight in her tone carried through the store. He hesitated before approaching, his boots echoing faintly across the linoleum.

When he reached her, she didn't look up. "When you arrived," she asked, "did you see anything around the victim's neck?"

Colton shifted his stance. "Yes, ma'am," he said finally. "There was something… a cord, I think. Why?"

"Because it's gone," Brenda replied, lifting her eyes to his. "Did you remove it, or did anyone else come through after I stepped out front?"

The question hung between them. He didn't answer right away. Instead, he rubbed a hand across his jaw and glanced toward the doorway.

"Detective," he murmured, "you'll have to speak with the Sheriff."

Brenda blinked, caught off guard. "The Sheriff?"

He nodded once. That was all he would give her.

Brenda stepped back from the body, her thoughts a tangle of unease and curiosity. Why would Sheriff Harper insert himself into a scene like this—and why remove evidence? As she left the store, the autumn air met her like a slap.

The drive to the Sheriff's Office was quiet but relentless, her mind looping the same question: *What could Harper possibly be hiding?*

When she arrived, she parked beneath the streetlight, its glow fractured by the wind-blown branches above. Inside, the building was hushed—too hushed. She walked past the dispatcher without a word and pushed open Harper's door.

He was at his desk, the lamplight casting deep shadows across his face.

"Sheriff Harper," she began, each word deliberate. "Why did you remove evidence from my crime scene and send Officer Colton to deflect my questions? What do you know about this victim?"

Harper didn't answer immediately. He leaned back in his chair, studying her as if weighing how much truth she could bear. Finally, he sighed.

"Detective Wisely," he said quietly, "I'm not concealing evidence. I told Colton to send you here because he doesn't understand what this case connects to."

Brenda folded her arms. "Then help me understand."

He nodded toward the chair across from his desk. "You'll want to sit."

Reluctantly, she did. The leather was cold beneath her hands.

"There's a case you haven't reviewed," Harper said. "You haven't seen it because I removed it from the cold case files years ago."

Brenda's brows drew together. "You *removed* a file? Why would you do that?"

Harper's eyes drifted to the window, where rain had begun to streak the glass. "Because it involved my son."

Her pulse quickened. "Your son? Sheriff, if your son was a suspect—"

He cut her off. "He wasn't a suspect. He was the victim."

The air in the room seemed to still. Brenda stared at him, words momentarily lost.

"Twenty-eight years ago," Harper continued, his voice raw, "my boy was found in a field—unconscious, barely breathing. He lingered in a coma for years."

Brenda softened. "I'm sorry."

He nodded, eyes fixed on something only he could see. "When he finally woke, he began to remember pieces. Names. Voices. What happened to him out there. And then, before he could tell us everything, he was murdered. In his hospital bed."

Brenda's throat tightened. "You're saying someone finished what they started?"

"That's right," he said. "And we never caught them."

"Then why now?" she asked. "Why bring this up with this case?"

Harper leaned forward, the light catching the wear in his face. "Because the man you found tonight had a rope around his neck—the same kind my son was found with."

She frowned. "That's a grim coincidence, Sheriff, but—"

"There's more," he interrupted. "Your victim had a playing card in his back pocket. So did my son. I had Colton remove both before anyone saw."

Brenda felt her temper rise. "You tampered with my scene."

"I protected it," Harper said evenly. "You don't understand, Brenda—this isn't just one murder. There have been eleven over the past forty-five years. All with the same markings. The rope. The card. My son was the only one who ever lived long enough to talk."

He paused, his voice hollow. "And when he did, they silenced him."

Brenda said nothing. The wind rattled the windowpane. Somewhere down the hall, a clock ticked past midnight.

Harper leaned back, closing his eyes. "Whatever this is, Detective—it's not over."

And Brenda, sitting there beneath the dim light of his office, realized the Sheriff was right. It wasn't over. It had only just begun.

Brenda stepped out of the Sheriff's office with the taste of unease lingering like copper in her mouth. The air outside was cooler now; the storm had broken fully. Rain whispered across the asphalt in a steady rhythm, hissing against her coat as she walked to her car.

She sat behind the wheel for a long time before starting the engine. The wipers swept across the windshield, revealing the faint outline of the station behind her—its windows glowing dimly through the curtain of rain.

A rope. A playing card. Eleven victims. Forty-five years.

Harper's words played in her mind like a broken reel. Each fact felt like a small, sharp edge cutting into something she thought she understood.

Back at her office, the hum of the fluorescent light was the only sound to greet her. The scent of old paper and stale coffee lingered in the air. She tossed her coat onto the back of the chair and sat at her desk. The surface was cluttered with files—open cases, pending reports—but her eyes found the old metal drawer at the bottom, the one that stuck whenever she pulled it too far.

Inside were the cold cases she'd spent the last six months dissecting. The names blurred together—victims who had once been whispered about and then forgotten. Until tonight.

She began flipping through the files, each folder a ghost.

Marjorie Hale, 1983 – strangulation.
Thomas Lattimore, 1990 – found in a creek bed.
Unknown female, 2004 – no next of kin.

Every one of them, the same pattern: ligature marks around the neck. No clear motive. No suspect. No closure.

Brenda traced her finger along the edge of a faded photograph—a crime scene shot from 1990. The victim's body lay in tall grass, the rope still visible, frayed at one end.

Her heart began to pound. The texture of the rope—thick, uneven—wasn't commercial grade. It was handmade, the kind used in older agricultural work, the kind rarely seen anymore.

"Who the hell keeps something like this for forty years?" she whispered to herself.

Lightning flared outside, throwing her reflection across the office window—a ghostly silhouette surrounded by file boxes.

She stood and crossed to the evidence board. Red pins marked each location where the victims had been found. The pattern had always seemed random—until she looked again.

The pins weren't scattered. They curved.

A slow, deliberate crescent that followed the old highway out of town—ending in the field where the Sheriff's son had been found.

Brenda's throat tightened.

She grabbed her phone, dialing the Sheriff's direct line. It rang once before going to voicemail. She hesitated, then hung up. If she was right, if the pattern meant what she thought it did, then whoever had started this had never stopped.

She glanced back at the newest crime scene photo—the victim from tonight. The rope. The card.

The Ace of Spades.

Brenda's eyes lingered on the image, the black spade catching the light in a way that felt deliberate, mocking. She reached for the box labeled "Unclassified Evidence," where she stored items from cases that didn't fit anywhere else. Inside, buried beneath old photographs and misplaced reports, was another playing card—also an Ace of Spades.

Her stomach dropped.

She hadn't noticed it before. It had come in with a set of unsorted files from the early eighties. No notation, no record of origin. Just a card, creased and stained, with a faint fingerprint smudge across the corner.

She turned it over.

On the back, in fading blue ink, was a single word scrawled by hand: "Survivor."

The storm outside deepened, thunder rolling low across the hills.

Brenda stared at the card until the edges blurred. Then she picked up the phone again—this time not for the Sheriff, but for the forensics lab.

"Get me a print comparison," she said, her voice steady but low. "On everything we have from tonight's scene. I want it matched against this."

When she hung up, the office felt heavier. Somewhere beyond the rain, a train horn moaned in the distance—slow, hollow, and lonely.

Brenda leaned back in her chair, her pulse finally slowing, though her thoughts refused to still.

If Harper was right—if these deaths stretched back nearly half a century—then the killer wasn't gone.

He was waiting.

Chapter 2

The Mysterious Letter

Brenda had been reviewing the ten case files Sheriff Harper had given her to investigate. The files could contain clues about what happened to her current victim, Raymond Johnson. While Raymond was a known local of Whispering Pines, not many of the residents of Whispering Pines knew much about him or his family, which was hard for Brenda to accept. She lived in Whispering Pines for over a year and learned a lot about many of the residents. Brenda found out most of her information about the residents from her friend, Emily Ross, who helped her settle in Whispering Pines.

Emily was a lifelong resident of Whispering Pines and knew a lot about the locals. Brenda's nosey neighbor, Joy, moved out of her home a month after Brenda moved to town. Joy and her husband built a house beyond the city limits but still in the county. When it was finished, they sold their home to Emily. Brenda, being a good neighbor, went over to Emily's house to welcome her to the neighborhood and introduce herself. That was the day Brenda felt a connection with Emily, so the two became good friends. They respected each other's privacy, unlike Joy, which was one thing Brenda liked about Emily.

After reviewing the files provided by Sheriff Harper, she decided it was time to seek information from her friend and neighbor, Emily. Brenda called Emily and asked if she would come over to review a new case. Emily excitedly accepted.

Emily was knocking at Brenda's door in a matter of minutes.

"Thank you for coming over, Emily. Please come in. Would you like anything to drink?" Brenda greeted Emily, who declined the offer from Brenda and made her way into the sitting room.

When they both were seated, Brenda took out two files from her office and placed them on the coffee table.

"Okay, Brenda, what do you have for me today? Who are you needing information about this time?" Emily enthusiastically asked.

"I am glad you asked. Keep in mind, these cases are old, and I am not sure how much information you may have on them, but I thought I would give it a shot." Brenda prepares Emily for her expectations of her knowledge.

"No problem, Brenda. If there is a chance I know something I have to try," Emily accepts the challenge given to her by Brenda.

"The first one here was a little over forty years ago. If you are ready, let's begin," Brenda tells Emily.

"Okay. Are we looking at the victim or the suspect in this case?"

"This one is about the victim. Do you know anything about a teenager from Willow Pines who was found dead in a field forty years ago, named James Turner?"

"Well, that was a little before my time, but I do remember hearing about him when I was in school here. I went to school with a nephew of his, if I'm not mistaken. I believe his name was Tucker Wilson, but I heard he passed away a few years before we graduated."

"Which leads me to the second case, the one about Tucker Wilson," Brenda quickly draws a link between the two murders.

"Wow, are you serious? Why are you investigating their deaths? From what I remember, both died in accidents. I remember Tucker telling people his uncle died in a farming accident in some field. Tucker also died in a farming accident, which, when you live in a farming town, accidents happen. Do you think their deaths are related to each other?"

"Well, because they are related and both died in farming accidents, I believe it may be possible they are linked together. What was their family like for either of them?"

"Well, I didn't know James Turner's family at all since they lived in Willow Pines, but Tucker Wilson's family moved here when we were in the sixth grade. The Wilson family were nice people, but when Tucker died, they moved away. I am not sure where they moved to. Being in Whispering Pines after Tucker's death was too hard for them, seeing that they had two family members die here."

"I can relate to their motive for wanting to move away. Who could I speak to about either murder?"

"Easy, Mark Thompson. He is a journalist for the Pines Times, our local newspaper. He has been there for several years. His father was a journalist there before him. If anyone knows anything about those two deaths, it would be Mark."

"Thank you so much, Emily! If there is anything else I need, you will be my first call," Brenda told Emily as she gathered up the files on the two cases while suggesting Emily leave.

Emily took the hint and told Brenda goodbye as she left, shutting the door behind her. Brenda needed to reach out to Mark Thompson, and she knew exactly how to get his attention. Brenda knew Mark had been following every case Brenda had worked on since she moved to Whispering Pines. Mark had wanted to interview her for several months, but Brenda declined each offer. Brenda thought this would be a perfect time to accept his offer of an interview as a ruse to get them in the same room together. Brenda wanted to interview Mark by making him think that he was interviewing her.

After Emily left, Brenda picked up her phone and called Mark. She told him she was ready for an interview but couldn't do it today and wanted to schedule a time and place for them to meet. Mark asked Brenda if next Tuesday at 10:00 AM would be a good time for them to meet. Brenda confirmed it would be a perfect time. He asked her if they could conduct the interview at her house to make her feel comfortable. Brenda agreed, and she ended the call. She now only had five days to gather more information about James and Tucker's deaths before her interview with Mark.

Brenda searched the internet for any leads on the Turner and Wilson families. She hoped to get more background details on both of the victims before meeting with Mark. Brenda wanted to see if she could gain some insight into why their deaths were classified as accidents and not murders, since Sheriff Harper suspected, they were connected to his son's murder. But she came up empty-handed trying to locate anyone in the families she could speak to about what happened. That was also suspicious to her. How could two families vanish after two members of the family died? Brenda wondered, acknowledging she had nothing new to bring to Mark during the interview.

The day had come for Brenda and Mark to meet at her place, and he was due to arrive in twenty minutes. Brenda made one last call to see if she could get something to bring to the table with Mark. She called Sheriff Harper.

"Sheriff, may I ask you something?"

"Detective Wisely, sure. What do you have?"

"I have looked over two cold cases you gave me from the ten, but I can't find anything in the files to suggest a connection to the other eight cases. Why do you think they are linked to the others? You said all ten cases were linked because of the rope around their necks and the playing card found on each victim. But I do not see any reports of a rope or playing card found at the other scenes."

"You are correct. Neither victim was found with a rope or a playing card. I felt these two cases could be connected to the others, mostly because of the type of 'accidents' they had. Don't you find it strange that an uncle and nephew both died in the same field where my son was found? After my son was found barely alive and then fell into a coma, I went back over all cases involving deaths in fields, and these two came up. Seeing as they were related in life led me to believe they were also killed by the same person. Don't you agree?"

"Sheriff, in both cases, no evidence of a rope or playing card was found on the bodies. While I did find some evidence that the other eight are possibly linked, I don't believe these two are. It is common for family members to inherit another family member's land after death, and that being said, they both could have died in farming accidents, as it states. Sheriff, both cases need to be closed as accidents and removed from your list of ten cases," Brenda expressed.

Sheriff Harper had a feeling deep down that those two cases were not connected to the others, but he wanted to make sure before closing them. He thanked Detective Wisely for her due diligence and encouraged her to continue investigating the other cases.

Brenda hung up the phone with Sheriff Harper and began to regret arranging the interview with Mark, but it was too late to stop it. Mark was scheduled to be at her place in under eight minutes, and she had no idea how to cancel it. That was until she thought about having Emily interrupt their meeting before it could start. Brenda frantically called Emily to devise a plan but was disappointed to learn she was not home. Time was drawing closer for Mark's arrival, but before she could think of something else, she heard a knock on her front door.

Brenda quickly walked over to her front door to answer it. She was surprised when she opened the door and found no one standing there. She did notice a note that was left on her door at the same time she saw Mark

Thompson driving up to her house. Brenda hurriedly snatched the note from her door and waited on her porch until Mark approached her.

"Detective Wisely, thank you for accepting my invitation for an interview. There is so much I want to ask you, and I know it will be everything the residents of Whispering Pines have been wondering as well. May I come in?" Mark expressed to Brenda as she stood between him and her front door.

Brenda shook her head quickly, as if waking from a brain fog. "Of course, Mark, please come in."

Mark walked past Brenda, went inside her home, and waited until Brenda was inside before taking a seat. Brenda closed the door behind her and motioned for Mark to have a seat, which he did.

"Would you like something to drink, Mark?" Brenda politely asked as she did with any visitor who entered her home.

"Yes, please, that would be great," Mark replied as Brenda turned and walked into the kitchen.

Once Brenda was alone in the kitchen, she pulled out the note that was left on her front door. It was written on a small blue piece of paper that could be found at any office supply store. When the note was unfolded, the first words she saw caught her a little off guard.

"The Tucker and Wilson deaths are not related to the other nine victims."

Brenda stopped reading the note and forgot why she was in the kitchen until Mark walked in behind her.

"Do you need any help with the drinks, Brenda?" Mark asked as he startled Brenda.

"Um, I'm sorry, but what did you say?" Brenda quickly wadded up the note she was reading and tucked it into her pants' pocket.

"The drinks. Do you need any help? You have been in here a while, and I was beginning to think you were backing out of the interview," Mark jokingly suggested to Brenda.

"Mark, I'm so sorry, but something has just come up in a case I am working on, and I need to act on it fast. I hope you don't mind if we reschedule the interview," Brenda told Mark without hesitation on her part.

Mark looked at Brenda, wondering what could have happened in such a short time for her to cancel the interview. He was perplexed by her actions but agreed to reschedule their interview. Mark said he would show himself out and left Brenda in the kitchen.

As soon as Mark left her home, Brenda took out the note she had found on her door and began to read it from beginning to end.

"The Tucker and Wilson deaths are not related to the other nine victims. As I am sure you have already figured out. Now that you are investigating the right cases, you are no closer to solving them. Focus on the people who don't want to be questioned, because the absence of light leaves nothing but darkness."

Brenda reached the end of the note, and while it let her know she was on the right track, it also let her know that not only was someone watching her every move, but the Sheriff's son's case was also connected. The note stated the other nine cases were linked, but she only had eight files with her, leaving the assumption that the ninth case the note mentioned was about the Sheriff's son. Knowing someone was watching her, she began to fear for her son Dalton's safety. She felt she had to fill Dalton in on her most recent case. She wanted to be sure he would watch his back and trust no one during this investigation.

Brenda waited for school to be over for the day to pick Dalton up and drive him home. While she waited outside the school for Dalton, she called Sheriff Harper to tell him about the note she had found.

"Sheriff Harper, I need to inform you of a situation that happened to me today. As I waited for Mark to arrive for our interview, I heard a knock at my front door. Thinking it was Mark arriving early, I went to answer the door. I found no one outside, but I discovered a note addressed to me stuck on my front door. There are some things in the note that lead me to believe I am being watched. The note stated, 'The Turner and Wilson deaths are not related to the other nine victims', the note says but while I have linked the other eight cases together, I am no closer to solving them. It also says I should 'focus on the people who don't want to be questioned, because the absence of light leaves nothing but darkness.' Does any of that make sense to you?"

"Nine victims? Are you saying my son's case is also linked to those eight?"

"Yes, sir. I believe they are referring to your son's case as the ninth victim. Now, does anything else make sense to you?"

"Not in the least. Are you okay right now? Where are you? I can send an officer to watch your back," Sheriff tells Brenda, who refuses to take another officer for protection.

"I am at the Junior/Senior High School waiting on Dalton. I need to let him know what has transpired today and make sure he is being cautious and aware of his surroundings. I will not tell him about everything, but I do need to let him know what I am working on because if they are watching me, they are possibly watching him as well."

"Understood, Detective Wisely. I know you will want to protect your family at all costs. If you need anything from us here, you have our full support."

Brenda thanked the Sheriff and hung up the phone when she saw Dalton walking out of the front door of the Junior/Senior High School. She quickly honked the horn of the cruiser to get Dalton's attention. By the look on Dalton's face, he was not happy with her honking at him in front of everyone.

Dalton walked over to Brenda's cruiser as quickly as he could to ensure she did not feel the need to honk again. As soon as he arrived at the car, he promptly jumped into the front seat and gave his mom a stern look.

"Mom, what do you think you are doing here? And why did you feel the need to honk your horn?"

"I am so sorry, Dalton, but something has happened today that I need to discuss with you. If I embarrassed you in front of your friends, I am sorry, but this is more important than what your friends think."

Dalton relaxed a little and began to lean back into the seat of Brenda's police car. He did not ask questions or say anything smart to his mom, allowing her to drive them out of the school's parking lot. Once they were on the road heading to their house, Brenda began to speak.

"Dalton, again, I am sorry about just showing up like that and honking the horn in front of your friends, but as I stated earlier, this is important. I need to let you know that you could be being watched. I don't want you to worry about it, just keep an eye out for anything suspicious you might see," Brenda explained to Dalton.

Dalton did not say anything back; he wanted his mom to continue telling him about what was going on.

"Now that I have your full attention, I don't think you are in any danger, but I want you to be careful when away from home. The reason I am telling you this is because, today, while I was waiting for a reporter for an interview, someone came up to our door, placed a note on our door addressed to me, and even knocked on the front door before leaving without a trace. The note had to do with several new cases I am working on. It did know a few things no one could have known unless they were watching me. So, you may not be being watched, but just in case…"

"Yes, mother, I know. You want me to be safe, and to make sure I know my surroundings. We have been through this before, remember? Back in Atlanta, that one case you were working on, and you felt I was in danger, but I never was. I appreciate the heads up, but since then, I have always made sure I was aware of who was around me and if anyone shouldn't be around me. Don't worry, I will be fine. I hope you will be aware of your surroundings," Dalton told his mom after he suddenly cut her off from what she was about to say to him.

While Brenda felt Dalton knew the most important parts of what happened today, she did leave out the fact that there were nine teenage victims whose cases were connected. One being the Sheriff's son.

Chapter 3

Patterns of the Past

Now that Brenda had been able to remove two cases from the other nine cases, she began to put together victim profiles for each of the nine teenage victims. She started with where the victims lived at the time of their deaths and where their bodies were found. Then Brenda moved on to comparing the age and sex of each victim, seeing if she could find a pattern of these children being selected or if their murders were just random. Next, she moved on to each victim's religious beliefs. She wanted to see if they attended the same church or even had the same religion. The last part of the victim profiles she looked into was to see if the victims or their families were connected in any way. Did any of the victim's family work at the same places, or were they part of any local clubs together? It didn't take long before she began to see some patterns arise.

Brenda pieced together the victims who were chosen and determined it was not by random selection. After reviewing the first victim's case, which was a male, she noticed the second victim was a female. This pattern continued with a male and then a female being selected and murdered. Each victim's body was found in fields around Whispering Pines, including the Sheriff's son, who was found in the Tucker/Wilson family field. She was also able to determine that three of the nine victims were from Whispering Pines, two male victims and one female. One of the male victims was Sheriff Harper's son, the other was the current victim found behind the store the other day. The female victim was the daughter of a local pastor who moved his family away from Whispering Pines shortly after her body was found in 1992. The other victims were from neighboring counties of Whispering Pines, and each was a male and then a female victim.

Now, with all these details connecting the victims, Brenda realized the person who left the note on her door was correct. She was no closer to solving any of these cases. Brenda knew she had to dig deeper into each victim if she wanted to get to the truth of why these children were selected and why they had to die. Nothing made sense to Brenda, which only made her more determined to find out the truth. By her calculations, since there were nine victims and the most recent victim was a male from Whispering Pines, a female victim from Whispering Pines could soon be selected and murdered as well. Brenda's only question about the most recent victim was why his body was found behind the convenience store in town and not in a field. This body disposal was a deviation from the past victims, who were all found in a field.

Brenda felt it was time to speak to Sheriff Harper and fill him in on what she had uncovered up to this point. She also wanted to speak to the Sheriff to get more information about his son. She knew talking with the Sheriff would not be easy because not many parents want to relive the events tied to their child's death, but she knew she had to press on. Brenda decided to call the Sheriff.

"Sheriff Harper, I think it is time for us to talk. Do you have time today?"

"Detective Wisely, of course. I have time to talk with you. Have you found out anything new about the cases I gave you?"

"I have. That is why we need to talk. What time is good for you?"

"How about meeting me at my place in about an hour?"

"Sounds good. See you then," Brenda ended the call with the Sheriff.

After ending the call, Brenda gathered her findings and the files and got ready to see the Sheriff. When she was finally ready, she grabbed the files and the findings and left her house.

While driving to the Sheriff's house, Brenda kept thinking about the questions she would ask him about his son. She was worried that if she asked the wrong question, the Sheriff could shut down and wouldn't answer any of her questions. Brenda knew she had to tread lightly. She needed him to know she was not there to judge him or his son but to get to the bottom of these cases. Besides, he was the one who kept all the files and had Officer Collins remove evidence from the recent crime scene. She also knew she needed to remind him that he was the one who knew all these crimes were connected. By the time she arrived at Sheriff Harper's home, she already had the questions in the back of her mind that she would be asking him.

Brenda pulled into the Sheriff's driveway, parked beside his duty car, and exited her vehicle with all her documents. She walked up to the Sheriff's front door, where he greeted her.

"Detective Wisely, thank you for meeting me here. As I said earlier about these cases, the group responsible for these murders could be connected with our office. I felt this would be the safest place to meet to discuss what you have uncovered," Sheriff Harper explained to Brenda.

"I remember, sir. May we go in so we can discuss the cases more?" Brenda quickly asked the Sheriff.

"Of course, please come in," Sheriff Harper offered Brenda.

Brenda followed the Sheriff into his home and took a seat in the living room. Sheriff Harper sat across from Detective Wisely in a large sitting chair. Once they were both settled, Brenda began to ask the Sheriff questions.

"Sheriff, I am here to tell you what I have uncovered and to speak to you about your son. I know this may be hard for you, but it pertains to the cases." Brenda prepared her boss.

Sheriff Harper looked at Detective Wisely and acknowledged that he was okay with her questions.

"Thank you, sir. First, I can tell you these cases are connected, not only because of the rope and the playing cards found on the victims, but also because there is a pattern of the victims being selected based on their age and sex. You see, they were all the same age when abducted but were different ages when found. Also, there is always a male, then a female, victim found in a field, except for this last victim. He was found behind the convenience store the other day, which is a deviation from the other victims. That leads me to believe there has been a change in the group that is responsible for each of these murders. Now, before we get into the manner of the last victim, let's go back to the male and female pattern. You see, a male victim was found first, then a female victim was found a few years later. Then, another male victim was found in a field, and a few years later, a female victim was found in a field as well. All of the other victims were found in the same pattern, a male, then a female," Brenda began telling the Sheriff of her findings.

Sheriff Harper took in everything Detective Wisely was telling him and began to realize he had missed this part of the pattern, which disturbed him.

"How could I have missed something so obvious, Detective Wisely? I had been investigating these cases for so many years, yet this was overlooked, even by me," Sheriff Harper began to question his ability to work a case.

"Sheriff, it was not easy for me to find at first. You may not have been looking for the same similarities in these cases. Anyone could have missed it. Don't be so hard on yourself," Brenda quickly tried to comfort the Sheriff.

Brenda gave the Sheriff a few minutes to compose himself before she continued.

"Sheriff Harper, I must ask you some questions about your son. From what I was able to gather from the police reports in his file, I see you reported him missing in 1995, and his body was found in the field in early 1996. I can assume the pastor's daughter, who was found in 1992, was the female from Whispering Pines to complete that part of the pattern. Knowing that, do you know if your son was religious? Did either of you attend church regularly?"

"Well, now that you mention it, no. We did not attend church ever. But he spoke more about religion the year before he was found in the field. He began asking me questions about life after death and if I believed we all went to heaven or hell, or if we just died. Honestly, I never knew what to say to his questions. So, I told him he needed to find out those answers on his own since I was not a religious person. His questions stopped, so I assumed he found someone else to talk to about faith and such. I never knew if he was talking to anyone about it or if he just stopped questioning things like that. Why do you ask?"

"I only ask because I do not have any religious background on any of the victims. So, I figured I would ask you first before I began questioning anyone who knew the other victims about their beliefs. I hope you can understand," Brenda replied to Sheriff Harper.

"Understood. Do you think these murders could be part of some religious group or ritual?"

"I can't say for certain, but finding out each victim's religious beliefs would either rule out religion as a possible motive or confirm it," Detective Wisely explained to Sheriff Harper.

"Well, I think your best bet would be to work on the current victim since it is a fresh murder. The more you learn about him, it could shed some light on the person or persons responsible for his murder," Sheriff Harper instructed Detective Wisely.

"Will do, sir. If there is anything else I need from you, I will let you know so we can set up a meeting place to discuss these cases," Detective Wisely informed the Sheriff and excused herself from his home. She needed to get to work on solving the current murder.

Brenda left the Sheriff's home and returned to headquarters to speak to Officer Collins. She was ready to review the file he started on the current victim, Raymond Johnson.

Brenda arrived at headquarters and walked straight over to Officer Collins' desk.

"Officer Collins, may I see your file on Raymond Johnson?"

"Sure, but it does not have a lot of information in it yet. I only found the victim's name, date of birth, and the location where the body was found. I have not located anyone in his family yet."

"That's fine. I don't mind searching for his next of kin. If that is okay with you."

"Please. Thank you, Detective Wisely, for your help with this case. I have never worked on a murder case, so this is new to me. I am willing to do anything you need to solve it, so if you need me, just ask," Officer Collins respectfully told Brenda.

"Thank you, Officer Collins. I may need your help later. I will make sure I reach out to you when needed," Detective Wisely reassured the officer as she took the file on Raymond Johnson from him.

With Raymond's file in hand, Brenda walked to her desk, placed the file on top, and sat in her office chair. After she was situated, she opened the file on Raymond. With little information in the file on the victim, she felt she had no choice but to reach out to Mark Thompson. This time, instead of an interview, she wanted to meet with him to see what information he had on the Johnson family.

"Hello, Mark, it's Detective Wisely. Do you have a moment to speak with me?" Brenda reluctantly asked the local newspaper journalist.

"Will this be our interview?" Mark quickly asked.

"No. I need some information on the victim found behind the convenience store on Main Street. Can you help me with that?" Brenda quickly clarified the reason for her call, and it was not about him interviewing her.

"That all depends on you, Detective Wisely. If I help you, will you agree to allow me to interview you on the record with a confirmed date?" Mark asked Detective Wisely with a hint of a quid pro quo.

Brenda took a moment to think about Mark's demands. She was not happy about being extorted by Mark to get some information.

"Fine, Mark. I will agree to participate in an interview on the record, provided that the questions do not involve my son or any ongoing cases I may be handling at the time of the interview. Do you agree with these terms?" Brenda gave her demands to Mark.

"I will agree to keep your son out of the interview, and I will agree not to ask you about any current case you may be working on. Do we have a deal?" Mark wanted confirmation from Detective Wisely before he would assist her in her case.

"Yes, we have a deal. What can you tell me about my recent victim, Raymond Johnson?"

"Detective, I said I would help you, but I don't have any information off the top of my head. I need some time to dig into the victim first. Can you tell me if there is anything specific about the victim you need to know?"

"Well, first, I need to know who his next of kin is so we can notify them of his death. Second, I am looking for his religious beliefs."

"Are you thinking his death could be related to religion?"

"Mark, I can't answer that question since it's about an ongoing investigation. I am trying to learn as much as possible about the victim to build a profile on him. So, can you find out?"

"Fine, give me a few days to see what I can uncover about the Johnson family. If they are a subscriber to the paper, I may be able to get an address for you of his next of kin. What will you be doing in the meantime?"

"I have my leads to follow, so you do your part, and I'll do mine. Let me know when you have the information I have asked for, if you don't mind," Brenda told Mark and quickly ended the call. She despised working with reporters of any kind because of how they portrayed her deceased husband in the Atlanta papers.

Mark had his instructions from Brenda. She now decided to reach out to someone who had helped her with Davie Youngblood's case last year, Ms. Carter, the secretary at the Junior/Senior High School in Whispering Pines.

Brenda thought it would be best if she went to the school in person to speak to Ms. Carter. She left the Sheriff's Department, jumped into her cruiser, and headed to the school. As Brenda drove, she thought about how helpful Ms. Carter had been during the Youngblood case and hoped for the same amount of help this time. Lost in thought, Brenda was surprised to find that she had already arrived in the school parking lot. She quickly parked her car, got out, and went through the front doors. Walking into the school, she reminded herself that Dalton was about to be a junior at this school and did not want to embarrass him so close to the end of his sophomore year. So, she quickly ran into the administration office, where Ms. Carter stood behind the desk.

"Detective Wisely, is everything okay? You ran in here so fast I assume you have an emergency," Ms. Carter quickly acknowledged Brenda's entrance into the office.

"I'm so sorry, Ms. Carter. There is no emergency. I just wanted to be sure I was in here before anyone saw me," Brenda explained to Ms. Carter.

"You mean so Dalton didn't see you here?" Ms. Carter clarified with Brenda.

"Fine, you are right. I don't want to embarrass Dalton this close to the school year ending," Brenda agreed with Ms. Carter as she walked to the counter where Ms. Carter was standing.

"No worries, your secret is safe with me. Now, how can I help you today?" Ms. Carter asked Detective Wisely.

"Well, I am here to see if you have anything on someone who may have gone to school here a couple of years ago. His name is…"

Ms. Carter abruptly interrupted Detective Wisely. "You want to know if Raymond Johnson ever attended school here in Whispering Pines, correct?"

"Yes, but how do you know that?"

"Easy. The death of a teenager in Whispering Pines spreads like wildfire. I had a feeling you would be coming to the school for information on him and his family. But we do not have any records of Raymond Johnson ever attending school here. That leads me to believe he was homeschooled, but we do not have any records of homeschooled children. Homeschooled children are not required to register anywhere, and, therefore, no records are maintained by the state. So, finding more information about the Johnson family may be difficult. Unless…" Ms. Carter stops mid-sentence with Detective Wisely.

"Unless, what, Ms. Carter?"

"Unless you can find someone who was friends with him, you may not find out anything about him," Ms. Carter explained to Detective Wisely.

"And how do you suggest I do that? How do you expect me to find out who the victim's friends were if we have no information on the entire family?"

"Easy, you begin to ask the rumor mill. There is nothing the rumor mill does not know about anything happening in Whispering Pines. I would start with a friend of yours that you trust. Do you know anyone in Whispering Pines who likes to gossip?"

"Yes, Ms. Carter, I do have someone in mind. Thank you very much. Now, I need to get out of here before the bell rings and Dalton or his friends see me here," Brenda told Ms. Carter while thanking her for her help and exiting her office and the school.

Brenda decided not to return to the office and chose to go home instead. She felt it was time to chat with Emily, her knowledgeable neighbor.

Chapter 4

The Old Diary

Brenda was unable to find out anything about the Johnson family from Emily. She was hitting one dead end after another, which frustrated her. She was running out of options to find Raymond Johnson's next of kin, much less anything about his friends or family members. Brenda was not used to not uncovering facts in the cases she worked. Just as she was feeling she had nothing more to go on, her phone rang. It was Mark Thompson.

"Mark, please tell me you have found out more about the victim on your end, more than I was able to find," Brenda pleaded with Mark.

"In a way, you could say that," Mark told Brenda.

"What do you mean?"

"I was unable to find out anything about your victim, but I did gain access to a diary of another teenager who was murdered. I think the murder of the person who owned the diary I found could be related to your victim. Do you think these two cases may be related?" Mark was on a fishing expedition, trying to gain more information from Brenda.

"You know I can't discuss a current case. But how did you find out about another possible victim?"

"Easy. I searched our archives here at the paper and found a female victim who was murdered and was found in a field. I assumed the victim was from Whispering Pines, since her body was found here. After finding that article, I decided to dig a little deeper. That was when I found out we, the paper, had the victim's diary. So I pulled it from our archives room and read it. There is something in her diary that leads me to believe that her case is connected to your current victim. Do you want to review the diary or not?" Mark bluntly offered to Brenda.

"Of course, I wouldn't mind looking at the diary. Where do you want to meet?"

"Let's meet at the diner on the square about four o'clock," Mark suggested to Brenda.

"Why the diner? Won't it be packed with people during that time? I thought we were going to keep our findings to ourselves until we found out more."

"Don't worry, there will not be anyone there at four o'clock. That is the dead time of any place in Whispering Pines. I thought you would have figured that out by now. You see, most older people are home, either napping or doing yard work. The younger residents of Whispering Pines are at their homes as well, but they are doing chores after school or homework. The middle-aged individuals are still at work, ensuring our complete privacy. So, four o'clock at the diner?" Mark revealed to Brenda how Whispering Pines works.

"Yes, if you say we will have privacy, then I will meet you at the diner at four o'clock," Brenda quickly agreed to meet Mark and hung up the phone before he could say anything else.

Even though Brenda did not want to meet Mark in a public place, she felt she had no other choice. Mark made it pretty clear he would only show her the diary if they met on his terms. She swallowed her pride and went back to the four female files she had on the previous nine murders connected to a group killing teenagers. She wanted to go through the females' files because she believed a diary would more than likely come from a female than a male. Brenda was unsure which victim Mark was talking about, being connected to the Raymond Johnson case, but she wanted to be prepared in case he had actually made a connection with one of the victims she had on file. If the diary was not from one of these cases, then she wanted to be prepared to either add a new victim to the current nine files she had or to find out how Mark had found a connection with the murders she was working on.

Brenda contemplated not meeting with Mark, but she felt that if she didn't meet him, she might never have the chance to review the diary he had in his possession. So she made a conscious decision to meet with Mark at the diner. Upon arriving, she noticed there were no cars in front, which suggested Mark had told her the truth earlier. She parked her personal car in front and went inside, quickly noticing Mark was the only customer there. He sat at a small table in a secluded area of the diner, away from the other tables. This made Brenda rethink her current position, so when she sat down with Mark, she questioned his choice of table.

"Mark, if the place will be empty while we are here, why did you pick a secluded table in the back corner?"

"Simple. I wanted to ensure we had a table away from others in case someone decided to come in. You know, like people who are just passing through. I wanted to make sure we were still able to talk without interruption," Mark explained to Brenda.

"Fine. Now that we are alone, may I know the name of the victim whose diary you have? I need to research the name to see if it is a case we have had here in Whispering Pines," Brenda asked Mark.

"Not yet. I want you to read some of the diary first. After reading it, if you don't feel these cases are connected, I will go back to looking for the family of Raymon Johnson. But I have a feeling you will want to peruse this diary in more detail before a decision is made," Mark reveals to Brenda, which piques her interest.

Brenda conceded to Mark's offer and asked to see the diary. She wanted to see what Mark was so worked up about.

Mark handed Brenda the diary for her to read the portions he had preselected.

Brenda took the diary and noticed the highlighter tabs Mark had in the diary, and decided those would be the first entries she would read. She thought they were the most important sections since they led Mark to determine that the current murder case was connected to this victim.

Brenda opened up the diary to read the first entry and was shocked by what was written.

November 10, 1992

I must say, the spiritual people I've met are incredibly kind and considerate. They are so welcoming of me and my past indiscretions with the Lord. They have already begun to forgive me of my sins. I always thought my past would forbid me from entering the gates of heaven, but I know now that I was wrong. My past is exactly why I will be welcomed into heaven.

November 15, 1992

Something has changed within the group. They don't seem to be as forgiving as they were in the beginning. Several of the elders have been distant and accusative of my past. I feel that they don't value me as much as they did before. I heard one of the elders telling another of the girls that they were going to make an example out of me. I am scared.

November 17, 1992

I don't think this group has any intention of looking out for me or even forgiving me for my past. I feel like they are using me as an example to the other girls here. I no longer feel safe and want to leave, but I'm not allowed. The Keepers are very secretive about my future with them, and that scares me the most. I want to do my part for them and go to heaven, but I don't think they actually want to send me there. I think they want to send me to hell instead.

November 20, 1992

Today I found out that tomorrow is my coronation. On one hand, I am scared, but on the other, I feel at peace. I have been assured I will ascend into heaven and all my sins will be forgiven. I find comfort in that. I know my family will be pleased with me for accepting my part in a long family tradition. All I have ever wanted to do is make my family proud of me, and tomorrow is my chance. Even though I am at peace with my decision to please the elders and my family, I know I must leave my diary somewhere outside of the Keepers of the Light's property. So, if you are reading this, I want you to know that I decided to fulfill my family's obligations to the Keepers. But I still want others to know I will miss them deeply.

As Brenda read the last entry in the diary, tears ran down her face. Brenda felt the fear through the written words of the person who wrote them. But, even after reading the diary entries, she was still not sure why Mark thought the victim of this diary was connected to her current murder case.

"Mark, thank you for showing this to me. But I have to ask you, why do you think my case is connected to this person?"

"Well, there is something I have not shared with you yet. If you will allow me to show you one more entry, I think you may find a connection," Mark told Brenda.

Brenda agreed and allowed Mark to show her another entry. As Mark took the diary back from Brenda, he quickly began to fumble through the diary until he found the entry he wanted Brenda to read. Then he handed the diary back to her.

Brenda took the diary from Mark and looked down at the entry. As she read the words, she could not believe what she was reading.

October 31, 1992

I am incredibly grateful to have found a safe place for my son, Raymond, and me to live freely without fear. The Keepers have assured me we will always be safe as long as we stay here with them, and I believe them. I want my son to grow up without fear of his father or anyone who would want to hurt him. The Keepers have assured me the Johnson name will live on forever since we are part of the Keepers of the Light. My parents are thrilled with my decision, which fills me with joy, knowing I finally received their approval about how my son was conceived. Thank you, Keepers. My love for you and my family will never be diminished.

Brenda understood now why Mark assumed this diary was connected to her current murder. The diary was possibly written by Raymond Johnson's mother four years ago. Upon realizing this new information, Brenda realized she had to explain how her current victim's name is in this diary without causing Mark to ask any more questions.

"Mark, before you start asking questions, I need to say something. Just because our current victim's name is Raymond Johnson, which is similar to the name in the diary, there is no way to confirm if they are one and the same. I will need some time to confirm if the owner of this diary is the mother of my victim. I can't find any information about Raymond Johnson's family, which is why I reached out to you. So, do you think you can set this diary aside for a moment and focus on what we do know? We have a victim named Raymond Johnson, and we have no information on his family here in Whispering Pines. While everyone in town knows of Raymond, no one really knows anything about him, not even the grapevine. You have to admit that it is suspicious. Since I moved to Whispering Pines, I can always find out information about anyone from gossip. But for Raymond Johnson, the gossip does not exist. I must ask, how is that even possible?" Brenda explained to Mark, who seemed to be just as dumbfounded as she was.

"Good question. How can someone live in Whispering Pines, and no one knows anything about them? Could it be that there are people who do know about Raymond's family but are not willing to speak about them? Like, maybe they are also tied to the so-called 'Keepers'?" Mark insinuated.

While Brenda had already come to the same conclusion, she was not ready to admit that fact to Mark of all people. She just needed Mark to continue researching what he could about the current victim's family while detaching the diary from this current case. She needed Mark to be able to separate the two things so he could figure out more about Raymond Johnson without bias. Mark agreed to leave the diary out of his research on Raymond Johnson and promised not to write about anything they had spoken about until they had irrefutable proof that the two cases were a mother and son murder by the same people.

Before Brenda left Mark at the diner, she had one more question for him.

"Mark, what is the name of the owner of this diary?"

"Her name is Jasmine Ferguson. Why?"

"No reason. It's just that I want to research any cases involving Jasmine Ferguson in Whispering Pines.

"Okay, do you need anything else from me?"

"Yes, one more thing. How do you know your diary owner is a murder victim?"

"Easy, the report I found in our archives headline was, 'Female Found Slain in Field has Been Identified as Jasmine Ferguson, A Missing Teen since October 1992.' So, I figured she was a local and her diary was found near a farm out on FM 1652, only a half mile from the field where her body was found," Mark replied to Brenda, who froze with surprise on her face, which Mark noticed.

"Why are you making that face, Detective Wisely? What do you know that I don't?"

"Mark, I am pretty sure I know quite a bit more about a lot of things you don't. But thank you for your help. I do hope the next time that we meet, you will have something on the victim and nothing more about a previous headline your father, more than likely, wrote back in the nineties." Brenda quickly uttered to Mark as she stood up from their table and walked away from him.

Mark was a bit surprised by Brenda's remarks but chalked it up to pent-up aggression from not being able to solve this case as quickly as she did in David Youngblood's case.

Brenda quickly walked out of the diner and moved swiftly towards her car. She could not get the name Jasmine Ferguson out of her mind because one of the nine cases she received from Sheriff Harper had the same name on it. The only difference was that Jasmine was not found with a rope or a playing card on her body. After hearing Jasmine's name, Brenda was able to conclude the victim was connected to Whispering Pines, so she began to wonder if all the victims had real connections to Whispering Pines that she had not been able to figure out yet. She knew she had to refer back to the information in the files instead of comparing things in the reports or what may be missing from the reports. Then she suddenly remembered something from the note she found on her front door. The part that stuck out was, 'Focus on the people who don't want to be questioned, because the absence of light leaves nothing but darkness.' Brenda was unsure why she felt this line of the note was about Jasmine Ferguson, but she had a gut feeling it was about her specifically. She just needed time to prove it.

Chapter 5

Uncovering the Society

Now that Brenda has been able to connect Jasmine Ferguson's murder to the murderous group attacking teens, to her current victim, Raymon Johnson, she needs to find his grandparents. To Brenda, his grandparents moving away right after their daughter's body was found, and not staying in Whispering Pines to look for their grandson, was suspicious. She began to wonder just how Jasmine conceived Raymond, because her diary revealed that her parents disapproved of the circumstances surrounding his conception. That is, until she was with the Keepers of the Light. Why would her parents approve of her situation only after she was out of their home and with a creepy group? Did something happen to Jasmine, causing her to become pregnant, or did she simply find herself pregnant from a one-night stand? Brenda wondered all of this to herself as she drove home from the meeting with Mark at the diner.

Brenda drove up to her house and, after parking her cruiser, she exited the car to make her way up to her porch door. She was excited to be greeted by Dalton, her son. She smiled at him, and he smiled back at her. As she walked inside, Dalton gave her a big hug.

"Thank you, Dalton. How did you know I needed that?"

"Easy, when you come home early and walk that slowly from your car to the front door, I know you are having a rough day."

"You know me so well, Dalton. I love you," Brenda expressed to her loving son.

"I love you too. Do you want anything to eat or drink?"

"No, thank you. I am fine for now. Maybe you can cook dinner tonight to ease my rough day even more."

"Sure, what do you want? Sandwiches or canned soup?"

"That's very funny, Dalton. You know how to cook, and you should know what I want to eat tonight, since you know me so well. I will let you know when I am close to being ready to eat," Brenda told Dalton as she rubbed the top of his head, messing up his hair.

Dalton quickly runs his fingers through his hair, trying to clean up what his mother had just done, before laughing and walking away to his bedroom.

Brenda giggled quietly to herself as he walked away and moved over to the living room couch. She dropped down onto the sofa and immediately got comfortable. She knew the next thing she needed to do was to dig into the Keepers of the Light, but she did not know where to start. Her only thought was to reach back out to Mark, the one person she did not want to talk to, the local reporter.

Brenda concluded that before she reached out to Mark, she needed to speak to Sheriff Harper. She needed to get information from the Sheriff about Jasmine's father, a local pastor who left town after her body was found, and why a grandfather would not want to stay in town in hopes of finding his grandson. The grandparents not looking for the missing grandson, or even reporting him missing, was the most intriguing to her. She knew, from Jasmine's diary, that they were aware of the birth of Raymond. Brenda also wanted to see if Sheriff Harper had ever heard of the Keepers of the Light.

As Brenda thought about the cases, she thought about what else she might want to ask Sheriff Harper about things he may, or may not, know about who worked in the Sheriff's office during Jasmine's murder. She hoped to obtain the names of the officers who handled Jasmine's case, as their reports omitted information about a rope and a playing card found on her. Suddenly, she was interrupted by Dalton calling for her, letting her know that dinner was ready.

Brenda set the file down as she was looking over on the coffee table and made her way into the dining room, where Dalton had already set the table for them to eat. Just as Brenda had suspected, Dalton knew what she wanted for dinner. She smiled lovingly at her son and then sat down to eat their meal together. They ate dinner, talking about how Dalton was enjoying his summer and how work was going, until they finished the food and were full.

Once dinner was done, Brenda excused herself so she could go to get ready for bed. She realized that she had a busy day ahead of her tomorrow and wanted to ensure she was well-rested.

The next day, Brenda drove to the Sheriff's office to see when Sheriff Harper could get away from the station so they could discuss the cases again. She wanted to gather as much information as possible from the Sheriff to reduce the time spent when speaking to Mark again. As she pulled up to the station, she noticed the Sheriff was pulling up as well.

Brenda parked her car, got out, and made her way over to the Sheriff's car. As she was walking up to his car, he got out and greeted her.

"Hello, Detective Wisely. What can I do for you today?"

"Sir, I wanted to see if you had some time today to meet with me about the other cases. Some information has come to light that you may be able to confirm."

Sheriff Harper took a minute to look around, to make sure there was no one around that could hear them talking. Once he was satisfied that they were alone, he answered her.

"Detective Wisely, let me go in and check in with the other officers, and if everything is calm, meet me at my place in one hour. You need to check in as well, and let's not leave at the same time. Will that work?"

"Yes, sir," Brenda told the Sheriff and went back to her car, acting as if she had forgotten something, thus allowing the Sheriff to enter the station first. Once he was in the clear, she began her way into the station.

As soon as she walked into the Sheriff's office, Sophie quickly called out her name.

"Detective Wisely, Ms. Cater from the school called for you. She left her number for you to give her a call when you made it in," Sophie told her as she handed her a piece of paper with a phone number on it.

Brenda took the paper with the phone number on it from Sophie, thanked her, and then headed over to her desk.

Brenda sat down at her desk and picked up her phone to dial the number that Sophie, the dispatcher, had given her.

"Hello, is this Ms. Carter?"

"Yes, it is. Detective Wisely, I presume?"

"Yes, I am returning your call. May I ask what this call is about?"

"Yes, I did a little digging into the background of Raymond Johnson and found something you may want to see."

"Really, what does it pertain to?"

"Well, his family, of course."

Brenda didn't know what to say to Ms. Carter. While she really needed to speak to the Sheriff, she wanted to find out what Ms. Carter had on Raymond Johnson's family. She had to make a quick decision on who she was going to meet first.

"Ms. Carter, when will be a good time for me to come by your place to see what you have found out, or would you rather come into the Sheriff's office?"

"My place is fine. If you are not busy, now would be a great time."

"Sounds good, I'll be on my way in just a few minutes. First, I have to speak to the Sheriff to let him know I will be out of the office for a bit. Can you give me your address?"

Ms. Carter gave Brenda her address before ending their phone conversation. As soon as Brenda hung up the phone, she made her way over to Sheriff Harper's office.

"Sheriff Harper, something has just come up, and I need to leave the office for an hour or so. Do you think we can discuss the other issue a little later this afternoon?"

"Absolutely, our discussion can be moved, not a problem. Does the current information have to do with your previous issue?"

"It does, sir. I will try to be as quick as possible. Thank you, sir," Brenda told the Sheriff as she walked out of his office.

Brenda went back to her desk and picked up a piece of paper on which she had written Ms. Carter's address before making her way out of the station and into her car. She drove quickly to Ms. Carter's home, hoping her information could fill in some of the blanks in Raymond's file. After a fifteen-minute drive, she found herself pulling into Mr. Carter's driveway. As she pulled up to her home, she could not help but admire the home. Her house was a gorgeous, white brick, two-story home on three acres of land. Her lawn was in pristine condition with seasonal flowers lining the front of the house as well as the sidewalk that led up to her front door. On her porch sat two rocking chairs and a bench swing hung at the end. It was a home one would see in a Home and Gardens magazine. Brenda parked her car in the driveway and made her way up Ms. Carter's manicured walkway up to the porch door.

Before Brenda could knock on the screen door, she was quickly met by Ms. Carter.

"Good morning, Detective Wisely. Thank you for coming on such short notice. Won't you come in?"

"Thank you, and please, call me Brenda."

After Ms. Carter opened the screen door, Brenda walked in and followed her into the sitting room, just off the kitchen area of her immaculate home. The two sat down in the sitting room, where Ms. Carter had iced tea sitting on the coffee table.

"You have a lovely home, Ms. Carter."

"Thank you, Brenda, and you may call me Katherine. Now, would you like a cold glass of iced tea?"

"Yes, thank you, Katherine."

Katherine prepared a cold glass of iced tea for her and Brenda before she began to tell Brenda what she was able to find out about Raymond Johnson. Katherine handed Brenda a glass of iced tea and leaned back into the large chair she was sitting in. Once they were both settled into their seats, Brenda began.

"Well, Kathrine, you asked me here to discuss some information you were able to find out about Raymond Johnson, correct?"

"Yes, it may not help you in your investigation, but you did ask me to contact you if I was able to find out anything about him. So, that is what I did."

"I appreciate that. Do you want to tell me what you were able to find out?"

"Yes, I was at my parents' home this past weekend, and I thought I would ask them about a child in Whispering Pines named Raymond Johnson. You see, my parents are very much in the 'rumor mill' groups in Whispering Pines. So, if I wanted to find anything out about Raymond, I knew I could ask them, and it paid off."

"Paid off, in what way?"

"You see, my mother used to go to a church where the pastor used to mention in his sermons how women who conceive a child out of wedlock were an unforgivable sin for a parent. My mom knew the pastor had a daughter who used to attend his services, but one day she just stopped coming to church. So my mom asked the pastor how his daughter was doing after one Sunday's service. She only asked the pastor the question because she had known his daughter from church and had not seen her in months, and he responded to her, 'Jasmine and Raymond are fine, they are with the Keepers of the Light, who will take care of them in ways we could never tend to them. They are so happy where they are, and we don't feel it is our right to interrupt their progress in salvation.' After the pastor made that statement to my mom, he just walked away as if they had never even spoken. She told me that moment always worried her about his daughter, Jasmine. My mom also began to wonder who Raymond was, since the pastor only had a daughter. My mom began to assume Raymond was Jasmine's child, the pastor's grandchild. Now, she was never able to prove Raymond was Jasmine's son, because as soon as Jasmine's body was found, the pastor moved the remaining family members away, out of Whispering Pines. I hope this helps."

Brenda took a moment to compose herself before speaking to Katherine again. She could not believe what she had just heard. Katherine's mother attended Jasmine's father's church and was even told by him about Raymond. Brenda was unsure how to respond to Katherine. Once she had all her bearings, she replied to Katherine.

"Katherine, thank you very much for this information. I really appreciate it. May I ask you something else?"

"Yes, please."

"Did your mother mention the pastor's name, or anything about the Keepers of the Light?"

Katherine quickly changed her facial expression from intrigue to one of concern.

"Why are you asking about the Keepers of the Light?"

"Because you just said the pastor told your mom Jasmine and Raymond were with the Keepers of the light," Brenda quickly responded to Katherine's mention of the Keepers of the Light.

"Yes, the Keepers of the Light were a part of the church where the pastor preached. We went to his church for many years, before they moved away, or so I'm told. I was too young to remember the church or its pastor. However, I remember that my parents took me to that church when I was a child. Before you ask, I want to clarify that I don't know anything about the church, Katherine began, but she cut herself off. Then she continued, "But I can meet with my mom again and ask her what she remembers about the church or the Keepers of the Light. Will that help your investigation into Raymond Johnson's murder?"

"Katherine, that would be amazing if you could find out everything you can about the church your parents used to attend. By the way, did your mother tell you the pastor's full name?"

"No, I'm sorry, she only referred to him as Reverend Ferguson."

"Thank you very much, Katherine. If there is nothing else you can think of right now, I must go. I have a meeting with the Sheriff later today to discuss another case. If you think of anything more about Raymond or Reverend Ferguson, please reach out to me. Also, let me know what your mother says about the church or the Keepers of the Light. I will be most interested in what the church had to do with the Keepers of the Light," Brenda told Katherine before she stood up and began walking towards her front door.

"I will contact you about anything I find out, Brenda. Thank you again for coming out today. It is always nice to have guests during the summer."

Brenda acknowledged what Katherine had said to her as she walked out of her home and to her car. Brenda was now ready to meet with Sheriff Harper so she could relay to him what she had just found out from Ms. Carter. She believed this information could link all the victims together. She began to think they may have all been connected to the closed-down church, Reverend Ferguson, or the Keepers of the Light, where Jasmine's father preached.

Brenda made her way back to the Sheriff's Station to get with Sheriff Harper to let him know she is ready to meet with him. She made the fifteen-minute drive back to the station and parked her car. Once she was parked, she exited her car and moved as quickly as possible to get into the station so she could talk with the Sheriff.

As she walked into the station and past Sophie, who was on the phone as usual, she walked directly into Sheriff Harper's office. As soon as she opened his door, she noticed Mark was sitting in the Sheriff's office. Seeing Mark sitting there, she was taken aback; she did not know what to say.

"Excuse me, Sheriff, may I have a moment of your time? I need to speak to you about an open case I am working on, so if Mark wouldn't mind leaving for a few minutes, I can discuss it with you," Detective Wisely awkwardly blurted out.

Sheriff Harper and Mark both looked at Detective Wisely with a bit of confusion. Neither of them knew how to answer her request.

"Detective Wisely, I can assume you know Mark. I can tell you he is here to help out with your investigation, if you will allow," Sheriff Harper related to Brenda.

Brenda was uncertain about Mark's potential contributions to her investigation, but she also knew the Sheriff wouldn't have involved him if he didn't have anything valuable to add. She looked over at Sheriff Harper and gave him a quick nod of approval and walked in and sat in the vacated chair beside Mark in front of Sheriff Harper's desk.

Robert Starnes

Chapter 6

The Missing Page

Once Detective Wisely sat in the chair beside Mark, the local reporter, she wondered how he could assist her with her investigation beyond what he had already accomplished. Since Sheriff Harper is the one who insisted on his staying, she felt she had no choice in the matter and knew Mark was about to get more information from her than he had so far, not for lack of trying on his part.

"Sheriff, I wanted to meet with you to inform you that I have received some information about a reverend who used to preach at a local church, before it was closed, and a group who was reportedly an extension of the church, the group was called the Keepers of the Light," Detective Wisely told the Sheriff and Mark, who was on the edge of his seat wanting to hear more.

Sheriff Harper took a moment to reconsider whether Mark should be in the room with them before replying to Brenda.

Brenda noticed the Sheriff's hesitation, "Sheriff Harper, would you like me to continue?"

After weighing his options, he replied to Detective Wisely. "Yes, please continue."

"Yes, sir. I have spoken to a resident of Whispering Pines, as I mentioned, there was a Reverend

Ferguson who used to preach at a local church, and it closed after he moved away. He is the father of Jasmine Ferguson, Raymond Johnson's presumed mother, but he moved away from Whispering Pines when her body was found. The Reverend's church also had an association with a group called the Keepers of the Light. Now, my source does not know to what extent the church and the group had to do with each other, but she is working on getting more information." Detective Wisely informed Sheriff Harper and Mark, whose expression showed that he may be able to shed some light on what Brenda had just said.

"Okay, but the information you have is just hearsay in a court of law, so do you have anything more?" Sheriff Harper informed Detective Wisely.

Before Brenda could answer, Mark had something to say, "Sheriff Harper, I hate to interrupt, but I may be able to fill in some of the blanks in what Detective Wisely said. Do you mind if I explain? Mark was prepared to inform the Sheriff and Detective Wisely about how he could assist her investigation.

"Please enlighten us, Mark, that is, if you don't mind, Detective?" Sheriff Harper quickly added to his response.

"I am all ears, Sheriff, please continue, Mark," Brenda replied sarcastically.

"Thank you. Since Detective Wisely contacted me to see what I could find in our archives about previous murders, I ran across an article about the Keepers of the Light. Now, I need to inform you that the article is almost forty years old, and it is the only time the Keepers of the Light were ever mentioned in the paper here in Whispering Pines," Mark referenced before he continued. "Now, the article I found mentioned the Keepers of the Light were a new affiliate for a local Baptist Church in Whispering Pines, and their focus was helping unruly children of God. It mentioned that if any church member had a child they could not handle, or a child that was falling off the path of Christ, the member could send their children to the Keepers of the Light, and they would get them back on their righteous path."

Brenda quickly interrupted Mark, "You mean to tell me that this group, the Keepers of the Light, was actually a part of Reverend Ferguson's church, and his own daughter was sent there? Not to mention that it is now apparent her child was sent there with her?"

"Detective Wisely, how are you able to come to that conclusion?" Sheriff Harper quickly interjected.

"Sorry, sir, Mark and I met earlier, and he informed me of a diary he found that belonged to Jasmine. In that diary, she mentioned she had a son named Raymond Johnson. That is what I wanted to meet with you about today, but before we could meet, I received a call from my informant, so I went to meet up with her to find out what she knew."

"I see, well, continue," Sheriff Harper sharply replied.

Brenda glanced at Mark, both waiting to see who would speak first. Mark chose for them both.

"Yes, I did find a diary of a victim who is connected with your current victim, Raymond Johnson. Her name was Jasmine, reported missing in 1992, and her body was also found in 1992. Her diary was found near the field where her body was found. Now, while I had let Detective Wisely read a few parts of the diary, there is a missing page from her diary," Mark told the Sheriff.

Brenda was unaware of a missing page, and she felt Mark was trying to withhold information from her during her investigation. "Mark, what do you mean there is a missing page of the diary? You never mentioned to me, during our meeting, that there was a missing page, so why are you bringing it up now?"

"Well, you seemed to be in such a rush after reading the diary, I didn't feel I had time to tell you about it, but since you are willing to listen now, I can fill you in," Mark intently said to Brenda.

"I won't get into law about leaving out information during a murder investigation, so please, enlighten us on the missing page," Brenda snapped back at Mark.

"Thank you, but like I said, it's a missing page, so there is nothing I can tell you about it, just that it is missing."

Detective Wisely was not pleased with Mark's answer and decided on a new mission. She needed to find that missing page.

"Sheriff Harper, do you know if the church where Reverend Ferguson preached is still standing? I know it was closed down, but you have not said if it was torn down."

"Yes, it is still standing. You pass by it every day on your way to the station from your home. It's the building with stained glass windows, a few blocks before you get to the square on the right. Why do you ask?" Sheriff Harper questioned Detective Wisely.

"Well, sir, I would like to search the old church to see if the missing page from the diary is there. It's possible that she left the page there, especially if it was about a group her father was involved with," Brenda suggested to the Sheriff.

Sheriff Harper quickly looked over at Mark, as if he did not want him to know of the possible whereabouts of evidence, like the missing diary page. He then told Detective Wisely, "I know the owner of the old church. You do not need a warrant to search the premises for evidence related to the missing diary page, because I own that property."

Brenda was uncertain how to respond upon learning that the Sheriff owned the property in question, which was also the same property as the church linked to two of her cases. She decided to keep her feelings to herself and accepted permission to search the property. Brenda nodded her head towards Sheriff Harper as he stood up from her seat and began her way to his office door. Before she was able to leave the Sheriff's office, Mark had something to ask.

"Detective Wisely, do you mind if I accompany you during your search of the old church?"

Brenda wanted to examine the scene, accompanied by another officer, before allowing any reporters in. "Mark, I think it would be best if I and another officer searched the church first, before releasing anything to the press. I hope you understand."

Mark was not pleased with Detective Wisely's answer, but he also understood her position. He knew that the press was typically not allowed at a potential crime scene until it had been searched and all evidence had been collected and documented.

"Understood, but will you at least let me know if anything comes up from your search of the church?"

"I will do what I can, but I can't promise you anything. It will depend on what, if anything, is found during the search."

Mark conceded to Detective Wisely and allowed Brenda to exit the Sheriff's office without any further interruptions.

Before Detective Wisely left the sheriff's office, she ensured she obtained a key from the sheriff to complete her search. Once she had the key to the old church, she exited his office and grabbed Officer Colton to assist her in her search of the church. She revealed to Officer Colton her reason for bringing him along once they arrived at the old church.

"Officer Colton, I have requested you to assist me in searching this old church because you removed evidence from the Johnson crime scene on orders from Sheriff Harper. So I assume we can trust you to be discreet during this search," Brenda openly told Officer Colton, who nodded at her in agreement.

Now that Brenda had confidence in recruiting Officer Colton for her search of the old church that Reverend Ferguson, Jasmine's father and her son Raymond Johnson's grandfather, used to preach before it closed down, she felt confident the search could proceed without incident. Once they arrived at the old church, they exited her cruiser and walked up to the front door. Brenda inserted the key the Sheriff gave her into the lock of the front door. Unsurprisingly to her, the door lock clicked, and she was able to open the door. The Sheriff really did own the old church.

When the old church door was opened, with a loud creak, Brenda and Office Colton looked at each other before entering the empty church. Upon entering, they both noticed how eerie it was being in an old church, empty, except for the pews still sitting in a row, the Bibles in the backs of the pews in front of the others, along with the hymn books beside the Bibles. It was as if the people of the church didn't just stop coming to the church, but as if they all disappeared from the church. There were layers of dust on everything inside the deserted church. But the more they went into the church, Brenda began to notice some spots where the dust had been disturbed. Not as if they were recently disturbed, but as if they were after the church shut down, meaning someone had been in the church after it closed. At first, she noticed what she thought were random places where dust had been disturbed on top of a few pews. But as she followed those disturbed areas, she discerned that they were leading to the choir room. Brenda continued to follow the path of disturbed dust. When she walked into the choir room, at first, she did not see any other disturbed dust areas, but she kept searching. She knew there was something in that room, so she kept looking. Brenda looked closely at the backs of the chairs, the books sitting on the table, and every item in the room. Looking harder, she quickly noticed a small area on one of the hymn books. It was a very subtle disturbance, but she was taking no chances of overlooking a slight disturbance. To her, any disturbance in the dust meant something.

Detective Wisely quickly yelled over at Office Colton and asked him to come to her location; she needed a witness to her findings. She did not touch anything in the room because she did not want to disturb the area. When Office Colton came in, she quickly ordered him to take a photo of the hymn before opening it. She felt she was led to that hymn for a reason. So, knowing that Office Colton had documented the book in question, she went ahead and opened it. But before she opened the hymn completely, she decided to perform something with the book. She picked up the hymn book, set it down on its spine, and let the book open on its own, hoping it would open to the page she was meant to see, which it quickly did. Upon opening, it was revealed that there was something inside the book.

As the old, dusty hymn book opened up from being set on its spine to two pages with another piece of paper between them, she and Officer Colton stood in shock. They were not sure yet what they had found. She expected it to be the missing page of Jasmine's diary, but of course, Office Colton really was not sure of why they were there in the first place. Before Brenda removed the piece of paper between the pages of the hymnal, she had Officer Colton take another few photos of their find. As soon as Office Colton finished the photos she requested, she took a pair of latex gloves out of her pocket and slipped them on before picking up the piece of paper from inside the hymnal.

Detective Wisely slowly opened the piece of paper from the hymnal and began to unfold it, when she suddenly realized it was the missing page from Jasmine Ferguson's diary. She quickly chose not to read it; instead, she asked Officer Colton for an evidence bag to place it in. She wanted to get it logged into evidence before reading it. She also wanted to wait and read it in full in front of Sheriff Harper and Mark.

Officer Colton opened an evidence bag and held it open for Brenda to place the missing diary page into it. After putting it inside the bag, Officer Colton marked it as evidence and secured it in the evidence kit he had prepared for collecting any relevant items for the case. When the page was in the evidence kit, he and Detective Wisely quickly began searching the church for any other evidence. They were both surprised, during a more thorough search of the church, that Officer Colton found several packs of playing cards sitting on top of a notebook. The finding of the pack of playing cards sent shivers down Officer Colton's spine, because he knew they were on the right track. He knew it was a big find considering Sheriff Harper had him remove a rope and a playing card from their current victim, Raymond Johnson's body, before Detective Wisely arrived at the scene.

"Detective Wisely, can you come over here? I found something that may also interest you," Officer Colton spoke out in the church.

"What is it, Officer Colton?"

"Well, I found a few decks of playing cards sitting on top of a notebook. I would like for you to witness the find before I take photographs of them so I can place them into evidence as well."

Brenda quickly made her way over to Officer Colton's position in the church, and as she walked into the room where Officer Colton was, she took a deep, gasping breath. She could not believe her eyes. Several packages of unopened playing card decks were resting on top of a letter-sized notebook with a black cover. She was mostly interested in what was inside the notebook, so she told Officer Colton to take the photos of the evidence he had found.

Officer Colton took out his phone and began taking as many photos as he could. First, with the items in the condition he found them in, packs of playing cards sitting on top of the notebook. Next, he began to set the unopened packs of cards alongside each other on the same table from where he found them, taking photos of each set of playing cards. Lastly, Officer Colton took more pictures of the notebook itself. Once everything was photographed and placed into evidence bags, he cataloged each piece of evidence in his log and then put each item into the evidence kit. The kit, which contained the missing diary page and the rest of the evidence, was closed, and Officer Colton secured the lid with a lock. Officer Colton then packed up all their equipment and began moving it from the church back into the back of Detective Wisely's squad car.

With the evidence and collection equipment all loaded in her car, Brenda walked out of the old, closed-down church and locked the front door. She was ready to return to the station so she and Officer Colton could examine everything they found inside the old church owned by Sheriff Harper. She was not willing to reveal any of their findings to Mark, not just yet anyway.

Brenda and Officer Colton did not talk on their way back to the station, but they both had a feeling of what the other was thinking. Both wondered how a church and its pastor could be involved with the murder of children, especially his own child. The thought sickened them both, children being murdered for a reason that was unknown to them at the time.

Brenda parked her squad car in her usual spot in front of the station. As she exited the car, she noticed that Mark's truck was still parked there. Knowing Mark was still at the station with the Sheriff didn't sit well with her, because what they had found was not meant to be seen by a journalist yet. If the information got out about their findings, it could jeopardize her entire investigation.

As Detective Wisely walked into the station, she walked quickly past Sophie, making her way straight back to the Sheriff's office. When she arrived at his door, she was surprised to see Sheriff Harper alone in his office, which made her wonder, *Where is Mark if his truck is parked outside?*

Brenda knocked on the Sheriff's door, which he instructed her to enter. She walked into his office, shut the door behind her, and took a seat in front of his desk.

"Sheriff Harper, I am here to inform you that we were able to find several pieces of evidence from your church, possibly pertaining to these cases," Detective Wisely tells the Sheriff as bluntly as she could.

Sheriff Harper was not surprised by what Brenda had just told him; in fact, he looked relieved.

"Thank you for letting me know."

"Sheriff Harper, is there something you are not telling me about the cases, or the church?" Detective Wisely felt his response was too calm for this information to be a surprise to him. She sensed he was hiding something from her about many things.

"No, Detective Wisely, I know nothing more about these cases than you do," Sheriff Harper replied to her, and she left it at that.

Brenda felt it was time to go to the evidence room and have the Sheriff join her to meet with Officer Colton. She was ready to find out exactly what they had collected. Her main focus was on the missing page of the diary and the notebook under the playing cards. So, she asked the Sheriff to follow her to meet with Officer Colton and talk about the evidence collected from the old church.

Chapter 7

A New Victim

The hum of the fluorescent lights in the evidence room filled the silence like static, constant and low. Detective Brenda Wisely stood over the table, staring at the sealed evidence bag that held the missing diary page from Jasmine Ferguson's journal.

The paper looked almost fragile enough to turn to dust. The ink had browned with time, but the handwriting still curved across the page with desperate energy — the kind of urgency born from fear.

What were you trying to tell us, Jasmine? What did you see?

She pulled on a new pair of latex gloves, the soft snap echoing in the still room. Harper stood to her left, arms crossed, face unreadable. Officer Colton hovered a few feet behind, his jaw tight, his eyes flicking from the evidence to Brenda as if afraid of what she might find.

She unsealed the bag with careful precision and unfolded the thin sheet of paper. Her heart drummed in her chest. The smell of age — faint mildew, old ink — rose from it like a ghost of its own.

When she finally began to read aloud, her voice trembled just slightly.

"November 4, 1992

I cannot believe I let my father talk me into coming here with the Keepers of the Light. They are not what they seem to be to the church community. These people are no more interested in treating us as much as they are in harming us. I feel that my life and my son Raymond's life are in jeopardy.

I heard one of the elders talking to my father and saying, 'Once the ritual is complete, you and your family will no longer have to carry the guilt of your daughter's sinful actions anymore. Once she is with our Lord and Savior, your family will be cleansed from her indiscretions and will again be welcomed into the House of the Lord upon her death.'

I think they are planning on killing me so my family can regain a place in Heaven, which is ridiculous.

How can my father allow us to be murdered to reserve him a place in Heaven? I don't know what to do. There are so many members of the Keepers of the Light that I don't know who I can trust. There are members from the Sheriff's Office, the school, the Mayor's Office, the City Council, and even more from the church.

Not only are there members from Whispering Pines, but there are so many more from every county around us. There is no safe place for us to run to for help.

This may be my last entry in my diary, because I am not sure what will happen to me or Raymond when I try to escape from the Keepers of the Light's compound tonight — but I have to try. I don't even know where we are being held, so getting away will be difficult, but I have to do whatever I can to save my son."

***

Brenda's voice faltered. The words hung in the air like the aftershock of a gunshot.

She stared at the page, her throat tightening. Harper had gone pale. Officer Colton's jaw worked soundlessly.

No one spoke.

Then Brenda swallowed hard and continued.

"November 6, 1992

I am so scared and don't know what to do now. I was able to escape from the Keepers, which was not far from Whispering Pines. The only place I could think of going was back to my father's church. We have been here for a few hours now, but I know we can't stay here long. Someone is bound to find us here, but I don't know where to go. God, I am asking you for guidance here.

I was able to reach out to someone from the church whom I trust, and I hope she will be able to get us away from here soon. She is supposed to come here and pick us up, but she is over an hour late, so I don't know if she is still coming. I pray Mrs. Carter comes soon, because if she doesn't come and we don't leave soon, this will all be for nothing and we could be killed.

I am going to leave this page here in the church and pray my father never finds it.

Just in case anything happens to us. But if we get out of this situation alive, I will come back and get this page, and you will never be able to read it.

God, again I beg you to look over me and my son during these tough times and protect us from the evils of the world my father is a part of.

Jasmine Ferguson and Raymond Johnson"

***

When she finished, Brenda lowered the page slowly. The air in the room seemed thinner now, as if every breath had to be earned.

Officer Colton spoke first, his voice breaking the silence like brittle glass. "Detective… this means there's a secret society operating here—one that's been hiding in plain sight for decades. The Keepers weren't just some church groups, were they?"

Brenda didn't answer. She looked to Harper.

The Sheriff's face was drawn, eyes glistening in the fluorescent light. He hesitated before speaking, voice barely above a whisper. "Yes. It's all true."

Colton blinked. "You knew?"

Harper nodded once, slow and heavy. "I started digging after my son died. I found patterns—names, locations. People in power. I didn't want to believe it, but the truth kept circling back to the same people. The same places. The same light."

He rubbed his temples. "That's why I asked you to remove the rope and the playing card from the last victim. I wanted to keep the investigation quiet until I could prove what was really going on. I didn't want the press or the townsfolk to panic. I didn't want the Keepers to know I was still looking."

Brenda felt her hands clench. "You kept evidence from the state lab. From me. From everyone."

"I kept it from *them*," Harper said sharply. "If I'd gone public without proof, they would've buried me next to my boy."

The room fell silent again.

Brenda looked down at the diary page once more, tracing Jasmine's name through the plastic bag. *You knew they would come for you, didn't you? And you left this behind, hoping someone would finally listen.*

"Sheriff," she said at last, voice calm but cold, "Jasmine mentioned reaching out to someone she trusted. Someone named Carter. She never made it out. But that means someone else was involved—someone still here."

Harper nodded. "Then that's where we start."

But Brenda didn't miss the flicker of something dark in his eyes—guilt, or fear.

Or both.

"I assume neither of you understands what's written here, correct?"

Brenda's voice broke the silence that had fallen across the room. She stood over the open notebook they'd found in the church, its pages thick with age, symbols scrawled in ink that had begun to fade into brown.

"That would be affirmative, Detective Wisely," Sheriff Harper said, studying the pages without touching them. "Are these instructions, or just scribbles?"

"To be honest, sir, I was hoping one of you would be able to tell me."

She closed the notebook softly, her gloves whispering against the cover. Before Harper could reply, Sophie's voice cut through the air from the doorway.

"I hate to bother you all, but there's a report of a fresh body found in a field out near Klienstown. Detective Wisely, are you available to take this call, or should I give it to someone else?"

Brenda looked up slowly. The words *fresh body* echoed in her mind like the toll of a bell.

"I'll take it," she said, her tone sharper than intended. "Thank you, Sophie."

As the door closed, Brenda turned back to Harper and Colton.

"If this is another one of theirs," she said quietly, "then they're not just hiding—they're still hunting."

****

The drive to Klienstown was a stretch of long, empty road framed by miles of dry field. The sky had gone the color of rust, clouds smearing across the horizon like smoke.

Brenda's grip on the wheel tightened. *If this victim is one of them, the Keepers aren't slowing down—they're accelerating. Less time between kills means one thing: someone's getting desperate.*

When she arrived, flashing lights cut across the farmland. A cluster of patrol cars sat at the edge of a plowed field. She parked, stepped out, and immediately saw a familiar face among the crowd.

Henry Brown.

A retired teacher from Whispering Pines—quiet reputation, rumored temper. He had been the landowner where Davie Youngblood's body was found the year before.

What are the odds?

"Mr. Brown," Brenda called as she approached. "I'm surprised to see you here today. Mind telling me why?"

Brown turned, his expression caught between smug and startled. "Detective Wisely. What a pleasant surprise. I'm fine, thanks for asking. How are you?"

Brenda didn't smile. "Very funny. I didn't ask how you were doing. I asked what you were doing here."

He adjusted his hat, eyes glinting with something she couldn't place. "Well, if you must know, this is my land. But I didn't find the body this time."

"Who did?"

"One of my farmhands."

"Then she's who I'd like to speak to. Where is she?"

"She," he said pointedly, nodding toward the fence line. "Over there."

"Thank you," Brenda said, walking past him without another word.

***

The farmhand stood a few yards from the body, her hands shoved into her jacket pockets, shoulders drawn tight.

"Excuse me," Brenda said as she approached. "You're the one who found her?"

The woman nodded. "Yes, ma'am. I don't know who she is. I just… saw her lying there. I knew she was gone."

"What's your name?"

"Tammy," she said, brushing her palms nervously against her jeans.

"Thank you, Tammy. How long have you worked for Mr. Brown?"

"Four years. I take care of his horses."

"Is that why you were out here today?"

"Yes, ma'am."

"When was the last time you were here before today?"

"Three days ago. One of the horses broke through the fence—I came to look for him."

Brenda narrowed her eyes. "And was the body here then?"

Tammy's head snapped up. "No, ma'am. I would've seen her. I'd have called the police."

Brenda nodded. "Just trying to establish a timeline. That's all I need from you for now. Please give your contact information to the officer over there."

She gestured toward Officer Colton, who was standing near the cruiser with his notepad ready. Tammy gave a small nod of relief and hurried away.

***

Brenda turned toward the field.

The woman lay face-down among the furrows, her clothing stiff and dusted with soil. Even from a distance, Brenda could see the rope.

Her pulse slowed to a dull, heavy beat.

No. Not again.

She approached the body carefully, the air thick and still. The grass around the woman's form was flattened, the soil disturbed. The smell of decay was faint—too faint for a long death.

When Brenda crouched down, her flashlight caught on something small and rectangular tucked into the victim's back pocket. Just a sliver of red against denim.

Please, God, don't let it be what I think it is.

She pulled out her phone, snapped a quick photograph, and slipped on her gloves. Then, with deliberate care, she reached down and drew the object free.

Her stomach turned.

A playing card.

The Ace of Hearts.

Another message. Another warning.

Brenda placed it gently on the woman's back, took another photo, and returned the card to the pocket.

Then she rose and called over her shoulder, her voice steady but cold. "Get the crime scene team out here. Full sweep. Secure the body."

Colton hurried to relay the order. Brenda watched the horizon as she stripped off her gloves, the wind beginning to stir the grass.

The Keepers are back. Or maybe they never left.

***

Back at the station, the world felt smaller. Fluorescent lights, quiet halls, the faint scent of burnt coffee. Sophie was at her desk as Brenda walked in.

"Detective Wisely," she said, glancing up. "The Sheriff isn't here."

Brenda stopped mid-step. "Where is he?"

"He went home right after you and Officer Colton left for Klienstown."

Brenda stared at her. "Thank you."

She turned and walked straight past Harper's office, heading instead to the evidence room.

The air inside was cool and sterile. The metal shelving gleamed under harsh light. She went directly to the section where the church artifacts were stored—the hymnals, the cards, the notebook.

Only the notebook was missing.

Her heart sank. She went to the logbook, flipping through the pages until she found the latest entry.

Checked out by: Sheriff E. Harper.

Brenda closed the log slowly, her reflection ghosted in the polished metal of the table.

Of course. You already knew what it said, didn't you, Sheriff?

She exhaled through her nose, the anger building low and steady. Then she turned toward the door.

If Harper had taken the notebook, then he knew something she didn't. And if he knew something—something about the Keepers—then she was done playing detective in the dark.

It was time to confront him.

And this time, she wouldn't be the one asking questions.

Brenda left the evidence room without a word to Sophie. She didn't want to sign out, didn't want a record of her destination. The Sheriff's house wasn't on official business—it was something else. Something deeper.

The cold night air bit at her skin as she crossed the parking lot. Her squad car waited under a flickering streetlamp. She climbed in, started the engine, and peeled away from the station.

You know what you're doing is against protocol, she reminded herself, eyes fixed on the dark stretch of road ahead. *But Harper has the notebook. And that means he's hiding something.*

The drive out to his property took less than ten minutes. His cruiser sat in the driveway like a silent sentinel. Brenda parked behind it, engine still idling. The front door was ajar, the screen door latched but not locked.

She knocked hard, calling out his name. "Sheriff Harper!"

From inside, his voice came, calm but weary. "Detective Wisely, please come in. And before you say anything, I can explain why I'm here."

Brenda pushed the door open and followed the sound of his voice. The faint aroma of burnt coffee and old paper hit her as she stepped into the kitchen—and froze.

The original notebook lay open on the table, surrounded by photocopies of several pages. Each page was filled with strange markings—numbers, symbols, and words written in erratic, slanted hand.

"Sheriff," she said carefully, "what is all this?"

He gestured for her to step closer. "We'll get to that. But first, tell me—this newest victim. Is it connected?"

Brenda hesitated, then nodded. "It is. The victim had a rope around her neck… and a playing card in her back pocket."

Harper exhaled slowly, the breath shuddering out of him. "So, another woman. Which means there will be a man next. You see the pattern, don't you?"

"I do," Brenda replied quietly. "And since we never released the rope or the card details to the press, it can't be a copycat. The Keepers are still active—and their pace is accelerating."

Harper nodded grimly, motioning to the photocopies. "Then we're running out of time. Look at this. I think it ties directly to the cards."

Brenda stepped closer to the table. Across the top of the page, a list of numbers and letters was scrawled:

1-10D (m & d)
1-10C (v & a)
1-10H (sof-l & g)
1-10S (d & j)
KQJ (l,i,p)
A (d & j)

Below it, a single line of text stretched across the page like a whisper from the past:

V kxiioo wkh fdugv dqg gudz rqh. Wkh fdug ghwhuplqhv wkh wshh ri vlqqhu zh pxvw wdujhw.

Brenda frowned, leaning in. "This bottom line—it's not English. Some kind of cipher?"

"Looks that way," Harper said. "I've tried running it through basic decryption tools. Nothing matches. The top half, though… that's something to do with the playing cards. You can see the suits."

Brenda nodded slowly, but something still gnawed at her. *This isn't random. It's ritualistic.*

She pulled out her phone and dialed Officer Colton. "I'm at the Sheriff's house," she said when he answered. "I need you to come here immediately. Bring your eyes, not your badge."

***

Twenty minutes later, headlights cut across the gravel drive. Colton entered through the unlocked door without knocking, per her instructions.

"Detective, Sheriff," he greeted, stepping into the kitchen. "What are we looking at?"

Brenda gestured to the table. "These are copies from the notebook found in the church. The Sheriff thinks they're linked to the playing cards. I want you to take a look and tell us what you see—fresh eyes."

Colton leaned over the papers, eyes scanning the coded list. Within seconds, his brow furrowed. Then he looked up, almost incredulous.

"Yeah," he said slowly. "This is definitely about the cards."

"Explain," Harper urged.

"Simple. The numbers one through ten with the letters next to them? Those are cards. The 'D' stands for Diamonds, 'C' for Clubs, 'H' for Hearts, and 'S' for Spades. The K, Q, J—those are face cards. King, Queen, Jack. And the 'A' is for Ace."

Brenda's pulse quickened. "You're certain?"

"Positive. I play poker online. I use a similar notation system to keep track of cards during the game. It's like shorthand for deck mapping."

For a moment, silence. Then Harper laughed under his breath. "I'll be damned. That makes sense."

Brenda shot Colton a curious look. "You cheat at poker, Officer?"

Colton smirked faintly. "You'd be surprised how much you can learn watching patterns."

Patterns, Brenda thought. *That's what this is—just another game to them. A game of sin and punishment.*

Harper slid the paper closer. "Then what about this bottom part? Any idea what that says?"

Colton squinted at the final line, lips moving as he sounded it out silently. "Vkxiioo wkh fdugv dqg gudz rqh…" He looked up, baffled. "I have no clue. Looks like gibberish. Some kind of code, maybe substitution. Are you testing me?"

"Of course not," Brenda said quickly. "You're the only person we trust outside this room. We wanted to see if it meant anything to you."

The tension in his shoulders eased. "Then no, Detective. I don't know what it says. But it's definitely intentional—there's structure to it."

"Thank you," Brenda said, her tone softening. "You've been more help than you know."

She glanced at the clock. 4:47 p.m.

"It's getting late," she said, straightening up. "I need to get home—Dalton's expecting dinner. Sheriff, do you mind if I take a copy of this page with me? I want to study that cipher tonight."

Harper hesitated, then nodded. "Take it. But not for long. We're going to need every hour we have—there'll be another body before the week's out."

Brenda folded the page carefully and slid it into a file envelope.

As she and Colton stepped out into the fading light, she glanced back through the open doorway. Harper was still at the table, staring at the notebook, his face half-shadowed.

You already know what it says, she thought. *You've known all along.*

Robert Starnes

Chapter 8

Ally or Enemy

Brenda walked into her house, and Dalton was in the living room watching a television show, which she was fine with during the summer. During the school year, she preferred that he not watch much television so he could focus on his assignment and grades. She greeted her son, but before walking into the kitchen to start dinner, she set a folder down on the coffee table, which had only one sheet of paper in it. As she set the folder down, part of the paper inside slid out just a little, revealing the last line on it. The jumbled letters on the part sticking out of the fold caught Dalton's eye, so he leaned over to get a better look at it. Brenda continued to the kitchen, not noticing Dalton's interest in the folder or that the bottom part of the page had slid out in front of him.

Brenda went about her business, preparing dinner for herself and Dalton, giving him an hour to study the paper from the folder she had put on the table when she came in. He had taken it upon himself to remove the entire page from the folder so he could look at it more clearly. He quickly understood what the numbers with a letter beside them meant but was perplexed at the other letters next to the numbers with letters beside them, so he focused more on the bottom part of the page. He studied the bottom page with the jumbled letters, which he quickly assumed was a full sentence, but could not figure it out at the time. However, after an hour of looking at the jumbled letters, he realized the jumbled letters were in a Caesar Cipher. A Caesar Cipher is a type of code that Julius Caesar used to communicate with his military; a simple code of moving the letters of the alphabet over three spaces. This was something they learned last year in history class at school, so he was able to decipher the sentence, but felt sick after reading it in its true form.

Once he knew the jumbled letters actually read, 'Shuffle the cards and draw one. The card determines the type of sinner we must target,' he called out to his mother, Brenda.

"Mom, can you please come in here for a minute? It's important."

"Can it wait? I am almost done with dinner, so whatever you want to discuss, we can do so at dinner," Brenda casually replied to Dalton.

"Sorry, Mom, but I don't think this can wait. It has to do with the file you left on the table."

"Dalton, what are you doing going through my case file? You know my work is private, even to you," Brenda shouted back at Dalton as she quickly made her way back into the living room. As soon as she walked into the living room, she could tell Dalton was afraid, so she rushed over to him on the couch and put her arms around him. She wanted to comfort him with whatever he was feeling.

"Are you okay? You look as if you saw a ghost," Brenda softly asked Dalton.

"Not really, Mom. Do you know what the bottom of that page says?"

"No, not yet. But we are working on trying to figure it out; we need more time."

"Well, I have saved you the time, because I know what it says," Dalton told Brenda with a tremble in his voice.

"What? You figured out the jumbled letters? How were you able to do that?"

"Easy, it was written in a Caesar Cipher," Dalton explained.

"A what? Never mind, what does it say?" Brenda quickly asked her terrified son.

"It says, 'Shuffle the cards and draw one. The card determines the type of sinner we must target.' Mom, what does this have to do with your case?" Dalton asked with a fearful voice, worried about his mother.

"Dalton, you don't have to worry about me. I am never alone, and I know how to protect myself. This is not my case; it is from an old case the Sheriff asked me to look into, so you have nothing to worry about. The case has been closed, but this part of the evidence was never understood. Thank you for figuring it out for us. I'm sure the Sheriff will be happy to know so he can put it all behind him," Brenda lied to her own son to protect him from her work. She never wanted her son to fear for her life or become concerned about her safety, but it looked as if she was unable to do that now.

"Now, let's put that photocopy back into the file and go eat! I am starving," Brenda playfully suggested to Dalton, to which he complied.

They ate dinner, having a pleasant conversation about the summer, things Dalton was doing to prepare for his upcoming junior year, and any love interests in his life. Dalton openly discussed everything his mom wanted to know, except his love interests. He was not seeing anyone at the time, and his past relationships were short-lived, so he felt there was nothing relevant to say to her. He knew if he ever felt serious about anyone, he could tell his mother about that person, but it had not happened yet.

After dinner, they both got ready for bed, and while Brenda was thrilled to know what the bottom part of the page said, she had to hold onto the information until the next day. She was not going to leave home that late in the evening to tell Sheriff Harper or Officer Colton, without drawing suspicion upon herself with Dalton. Since she lied to him, she felt it would be best to wait.

The next day, Brenda got up earlier than usual so she could leave home before Dalton got up. She wanted to avoid any follow-up questions he may have regarding last night's breakthrough on the Caesar Cipher he figured out. She was not prepared to answer any questions Dalton could have about the case. Brenda didn't want her son's mind to be corrupted by any case she might be working on; she wanted him to grow up without worrying about her safety as she investigates cases as horrible as Jasmine's case.

Brenda left home to head to the police station to fill the Sheriff and Officer Colton in on what Dalton had discovered. Now she had some information related to the page in the notebook that Officer Colton had found sitting under the decks of playing cards in the old church. Brenda pulled up to the station and parked her car to make her way inside. As she was walking up to the front doors, she noticed Sheriff Harper's cruiser was already in front of the station. As she walked into the station, Sophie was already sitting at the front desk, taking calls and dispatching officers to local addresses. Brenda nodded her head at Sophie to say hello and continued her walk to Sheriff Harper's office. Upon arriving at the Sheriff's office door, she was again surprised to see Mark sitting in the office.

Brenda gave a quick knock on the Sheriff's door before walking right into his office. As she barges into his office, Brenda quickly shuts the door behind her and moves to the open seat in the chair next to Mark.

"I hope you don't mind me interrupting your meeting, but I have a few things I need to say to Sheriff Harper. If you don't mind, Mark, could you excuse us?" Brenda sharply asked Mark before the Sheriff could respond to her interruption.

"Detective Wisely, while I am sure the information you have to tell me is important, I will allow Mark to stay. I hope you don't mind," Sheriff Harper replied before Mark had a chance.

Brenda was a little taken aback by Sheriff Harper's response, but also knew she could not deny his request.

"No, sir. If you want to allow Mark to stay, that is fine with me," Brenda conceded to the Sheriff.

"Great. Now that we have that out of the way, what do you have for us today?" Sheriff Harper asked Detective Wisely.

"As you wish, sir. My son, Dalton, noticed a file I took home last night, and since the photocopy of the page from the notebook slipped out a little, he noticed the jumbled letters on the bottom of the page. With that being said, he figured out what the jumbled words actually said. Would you like me to read the sentence in front of you and Mark?"

Sheriff Harper took a moment to gather his thoughts because it was obvious to Brenda that he was not prepared for her to say that she figured out those jumbled words. He figured she was going to update her on her day and what her next step would be in trying to solve the letters on the page.

"Mark, I am going to have to ask you to leave, if you don't mind. We will pick up our conversation later today. Thank you for understanding. You can see your way out, correct?"

Mark was surprised that Sheriff Harper so quickly dismissed him from being there because of what Detective Wisely had just told him. But before he left, he had to ask, "Sheriff, what was Detective Wisely saying about jumbled words in a notebook?"

"Again, Mark, I must ask you to leave. Please make your way towards the door before I ask Detective Wisely to escort you out," Sheriff Harper threatened Mark to make sure he got the point.

Mark understood the Sheriff's demand and stopped asking questions, got up, and made his way out of the Sheriff's office.

Once Mark was gone and the office door was shut again, Sheriff Harper quickly looked at Detective Wisely. He was ready to hear what she had to say now.

"Thank you, Sheriff. As I was saying, my son figured out what the jumbled letters meant on the button of the page from the notebook. The letters are actually a sentence that reads, 'Shuffle the cards and draw one. The card determines the type of sinner we must target.' So, now with Officer Colton's information about what the numbers and letters on the top of the page mean, we are close to being able to decipher the entire page," Brenda told Sheriff Harper, who was shocked by the sentence she said to him.

"What in the world could that mean? 'Shuffle the cards and draw one. The card determines the type of sinner we must target.' What does this mean?"

"I'm not sure yet, but I believe we are on the right track. With Officer Colton figuring out that the numbers with letters beside them on the top part are the numbers and suits of a deck of playing cards, and the fact that the jumbled letters mention 'shuffle the cards and draw one', we are on the right track."

"I agree, we are getting very close, but without knowing what the other random letters are beside the 'J, Q, K', we need to continue digging. I have a suggestion for you, but you may not like it," Sheriff Harper informs Brenda.

Hearing the Sheriff had a suggestion for her not only intrigued her, but also worried her. She never knew what was going through the Sheriff's mind, but she did want to hear his suggestion.

"Okay, so what is your suggestion?"

"Well, since you asked, there is someone else I think you should speak to. Now, this is someone who knows almost everything about Whispering Pines, meaning he may also know things that have never been posted in the paper. He is actually a local historian, and his name is Samuel Everest. Now, I am not suggesting you talk to him and reveal things we know about the Keepers of the Light but see if you can gather any information from him about them. Do you understand what I am saying?"

"I believe I do. You suggest I ask him questions as if he is an ally, but treat him as the enemy," Brenda responded to the Sheriff as she winked her eye at him. "So, where can I find Mr. Everest?"

"Easy, his office is directly beside the library. His office hours are weekdays from 8:00 AM to 3:00 PM. He is in his office every day, because he loves for anyone to visit him to talk about Whispering Pines."

"Thank you, sir, I will be on my way now," Brenda told the Sheriff as she stood up and walked out of his office.

Brenda found it interesting what the Sheriff said about Samuel, even more about how she interpreted how she should treat Samuel. She walked out of the station without speaking to Sophie, as she was on the phone at the time. Brenda decided not to drive over to Mr. Everest's office, since it was just caddy corner from the Sheriff's station. It only took Brenda a few minutes to walk across the street to Mr. Everest's office.

As soon as Brenda made it over to Mr. Everest's office door, she could quickly tell that he was very interested in Whispering Pines' history. His office door had posters and flyers from past events in the town. While none of his door hangings mentioned secret religious groups or murdered victims found in the county over the past forty years, she did notice one of the flyers with David Youngblood's photo on it. Seeing that flier on his door hit her heart with such sorrow, knowing what she knew then about what actually happened to Davie during the time of his disappearance. Yet, she felt she could try to connect with Mr. Everest because she solved his murder, so she quickly walked into his office to meet him.

Brenda walked into Mr. Everest's office and was quickly drawn to the items he had lining the walls of his office. Many of the items went back over a hundred years, which interested her as a newcomer to the town, and she even felt Dalton could learn a few things about Whispering Pines from Samuel Everest.

"Hello, Detective Wisely, it is finally nice to meet you formally. I have read a lot about you and how you were able to solve the Davie Youngblood case after ten years. That was impressive. I never believed he ran away; I always felt he never left Whispering Pines. So, thank you for your due diligence in his case. Now, what can I do for you today?" A slightly overweight, balding, older gentleman came out from around a corner in the room.

"Mr. Everest, I assume. Thank you for your compliment regarding Davie. I was drawn to his cold case as soon as I read his file. I knew there was more to his story, and I felt in my heart I needed to bring closure to his mother, June. She is such a lovely lady," Brenda replied to the gentleman in the office.

"You are correct, I am Samuel Everest, but you can call me Samuel. Do you mind if I call you Brenda?"

"Of course, you can call me Brenda. You know, this is my first time here, and I must say, I am impressed by all of your history of Whispering Pines," Brenda agreed to allow Samuel to call her by her first name, to build some rapport with Samuel.

"Thank you, Brenda. So, what brings you into my world today?"

"Oh, not much, but since I am new here, I actually wanted to learn more about things I wouldn't find in the archives of the local paper. Do you have any stories or history about things like that?" Brenda quickly laid the groundwork for how she wanted the rest of their conversations to go.

"Well, there are many things that happen in history that never make the papers. Sometimes the smallest events mean nothing to the reporters but mean so much to the people who they may have involved. You know what I am talking about, Brenda?"

"I do actually, Samuel. Those are the things I am interested in. As you may know, my son and I are from Atlanta, GA, and we moved here because of some horrible things that were being said about my late husband, God rest his soul. Because of all the things that were being said about my son's father, I decided to leave Atlanta and move here so I could try to give my son a better life, away from those awful things being said about my late husband. With that being said, I am wondering if there are any dark secrets about Whispering Pines that I should be made aware of, ones that my co-workers wouldn't tell me."

Samuel looked at Brenda with a bit of discomfort, like he had been treated that way before by a newcomer to Whispering Pines.

Brenda quickly noticed how he was taken aback by her question. She wondered how she could reword her question to put Samuel at ease a little. But before she could reword her question, Samuel replied to her.

"Brenda, may I be blunt with you?"

"Of course you can, Samuel."

"What are you really looking for today? I have no problem answering your question, but I want the truth from you, not some police style question I am asked all the time."

"I'm so sorry, Samuel. I did not mean to make you feel uneasy. I am just trying to get to know the town better. Really," Brenda tried to cover her tracks to Samuel, but he was not buying it.

"Brenda, I have been in Whispering Pines my entire life, and I have been questioned by the police many times since taking over as the local historian of Whispering Pines. I can tell when someone is beating around the bush. Now, just tell me what you really want to know."

"I get it, Samuel, you are too smart for me to try to manipulate, so I will be as blunt with you as you are with me. I am looking for anything you might know about a religious group, which could be from Whispering Pines or not, called the Keepers of the Light. Do you have any history with the group?"

Samuel could not believe what Brenda had just asked him. He had not heard that name in over twenty years. The mention of the group brought back a flood of memories from the past rushing through his mind. He started remembering the controversial methods the group was accused of using to help wayward children. He was not proud of his own involvement in the group, but he was not going to tell Brenda about his past.

"Well, that is a very specific request you have asked. Is there a reason you are asking about this particular group?"

"To be honest, I heard the name of the group recently at a friend's house. While I was attending a party at their house, I walked into a room in their home and interrupted a conversation between her parents. Now, I only heard bits and pieces of that conversation, such as Keepers of the Light and religion. When I asked them about what they were talking about, they suddenly stopped and changed the subject. Being new here in Whispering Pines, it piqued my interest. So, do you have any history of such a group existing in Whispering Pines?"

"As it just so happens, I do have some history on the Keepers of the Light. It is not much, but it is fascinating. Would you like me to retrieve what I have on them?"

"That would be great. I find it interesting how such groups could exist in a small town like Whispering Pines, but not in a large city like Atlanta."

"That's a presumptuous thought. How do you know they don't exist in large cities?"

"Only because I came here from Atlanta, and as a detective there, I had never had a case involving any religious group with the name Keepers of the Light."

"Well, I can assure you they do exist in many major cities, not just the small towns…" Samuel quickly stopped mid-sentence. He felt he was giving away too much information about the group he was pretending to know not much about. "Let me gather what I have on the group, and I'll let you come to your own conclusion about them."

Before Brenda could respond to Samuel, she took notice of his sudden stop about the group as he walked away from her to a back room in his office. She then understood what Sheriff Harper told her about Samuel: speak to him as an ally but treat him as the enemy. He obviously knew more about the group than he was letting on to her.

Samuel was gone for only five minutes before walking back into the room with a small box in his hands. He walked over to Brenda, set the box down on a desk in his office, removed the lid, and then walked away from her. He wanted her to review the material he had provided to her by herself. He didn't want to be in the room as she did so, to avoid any follow-up questions she might have for him.

"Brenda, this box contains the only information I have on that particular group, so take your time looking it over. I have an appointment to attend at this time, so when you are finished, please put the lid back on the box and leave it here. I trust you will abide by the rules here," Samuel expressed to Brenda before he walked away, leaving her alone with the information she requested.

Brenda was not shocked by Samuel's actions, as she had already begun to come to her own conclusions.

She felt Samuel knew more than he was going to reveal to her. She allowed for Samuel to leave, thinking maybe she could return at a later date, if needed.

Once Samuel was out of the room, Brenda began to peek into the box he had left for her. She was not surprised by the lack of actual information she found amongst the things in the box. There were some things inside the box, like a notebook that resembled the one Officer Colton found in the church with the decks of playing cards. Brenda removed the notebook, and as soon as she opened it, she noticed something she had seen before. There was a page with numbers and letters on it and a word in parentheses beside each one of them. She knew then she was looking at the key to decipher the rest of the notebook they had in their possession at the station. The page revealed everything they were lacking to understand what they were facing.

Common Children
1-10D (materialism & greed)
1-10C (violence & aggression)
1-10H (sins of the flesh, lust & gluttony)
1-10S (death & judgment)

Selected Children
K (leaders)
Q (influencer)

J (power in the community)
A (beginning and ending, severe punishment)

Brenda then knew how the children had been picked by the Keepers of the Light. She took a photo of the page with her phone before putting all the items back into the box so she could replace the lid on it. She wanted to respect Samuel's wishes and leave everything in the box, in the hopes he could eventually see her as an ally, not the enemy.

Once everything was back in the box and the lid was on it, she walked out of Samuel's office to begin her way back over to the Sheriff's station. She was then prepared to review the page in the notebook they had uncovered with Sheriff Harper and Officer Colton.

Robert Starnes

Chapter 9
The Keeper's Meeting

Brenda made it across the street and back to the station in just a few minutes. She saw Officer Colton's car parked outside, along with Sheriff Harper's cruiser. Seeing they were both at the station pleased her, because she was ready to let them both know what she had found out from Samuel. She felt they were closer to uncovering the entire group's mentality; that their selection of children was not only by choice or because a parent requested it, but it was also about chance. Now that she knew what the letters in the parentheses meant, she knew they were merely relying on a deck of cards to tell them what type of child to kill during that year's ritual.

Brenda walked into the station, stopping at the front desk to see if Sophie had any messages for her. "Good morning, Sophie. Do I have any messages?"

"Good morning, Detective Wisely. Sorry, but I don't have any messages for you. Are you expecting someone to call for you? Because if you are, I will let you know if anyone calls for you," Sophie sharply responded to Detective Wisely.

Brenda shook off how Sophie responded to her about any messages, while thanking her as she turned to walk to the Sheriff's office. As she walked past the other officers in the bullpen, she noticed Officer Colton at his desk and got his attention.

"Officer Colton, can I see you in Sheriff Harper's office for a moment?"

Office Colton was taken off guard by Detective Wisely's loud and sudden demand to see him in the Sheriff's office. He wondered if he had done something wrong, but nothing came to mind. So, the officer acknowledged the detective's request, met her in the hallway, and followed her to Sheriff Harper's office. As soon as they both arrived at the Sheriff's office door, she quickly opened the door to the office without knocking.

With the office door open, Brenda walked into the Sheriff's office with Officer Colton in tow. Once they were both inside his office, she took one of the empty seats in front of the Sheriff's desk, pointing for Officer Colton to take the other. When they were both seated, she began to explain why she had brought Officer Colton into her meeting with Sheriff Harper.

"Officer Colton, I have asked you to come with me here so the three of us can go over some things I have been able to uncover about the page in the notebook you found in the old church. Are you okay with being here with us?"

"Yes, ma'am. How can I help?" Officer Colton honestly answered Brenda.

"Thank you. Sheriff Harper. I need to inform you both on what Samuel Everest was able to provide me about the Keepers of the Light. I am unsure what made you think Samuel would have any information on the Keepers. Sir, how did you know Samuel would be able to fill in some blanks we could not fill with the notebook we have from the church?"

Sheriff Harper leaned back in his chair, shifting his weight from one side to the other, as if he was becoming uncomfortable. He locked eyes with Brenda before answering her questions.

"Detective Wisely, to be clear, I did not know for a fact he would be able to provide any information about them, but I did have a hunch."

"How could you possibly have a hunch about Samuel? You are leaving something out, sir. I need to know what that is."

"You are correct, once again, Detective Wisely. I have left something out, but it was only because my hunch was based on a rumor. Many years ago, a rumor was going through Whispering Pines about Samuel being involved with a religious group targeting residents. The rumor was that the group would take some of the older residents here for all their money. I never heard the name of the group he was rumored to be a part of, but I figured if anyone knew anything about the

Keepers, it would be Samuel, since he may have been involved in a group similar to the Keepers."

Brenda thought about what Sheriff Harper had just told her, and while his explanation made sense, she still felt like he was holding more back from her. She decided to push her thoughts aside so she could continue letting Sheriff Harper and Officer Colton in on what she was able to find out, based on the Sheriff's hunch.

"Understood, sir. Now, I did not remove anything from Samuel's office, but I did take a photo of something we have been looking for. It's the key code for the page in the notebook that we have been unable to figure out. I know what the letters in parentheses by the numbers and letters mean. Here, look at this photo," Brenda told both of them as she pulled out her phone and opened the photo.

Common Children
1-10D (materialism & greed)
1-10C (violence & aggression)
1-10H (sins of the flesh, lust & gluttony)
1-10S (death & judgment)

Selected Children
K (leaders)
Q (influencer)

J (power in the community)
A (beginning and ending, severe punishment)

"Now we know what each of the murdered children represents to the group. The children whom they murdered were chosen based on the card they picked from the deck. If they pulled out a numbered suit card, let's say the 10 of hearts, that means they would have picked a common child they deemed as someone who possibly had sex before marriage, or someone promiscuous, or a heavy child. Now, if they pulled out a letter card, such as a King, Queen, Jack, or Ace of any suit, the child was to be a more specific type. The child they picked would still be chosen based on the sin, but for a face card, the child would come from a leader, influencer, or someone with power in the community. Now, the Ace is still a mystery for me because I did not find anything in Samuel's things to explain what a beginning and an ending meant. But I can assume it was the most severe punishment they gave," Brenda finished bringing the Sheriff and Officer Colton up to speed.

Office Colton's face lost some of its color during Detective Wisely's briefing. He looked as if he was about to pass out, so Brenda reached over and put her hand on his shoulder. She was letting him know he was not alone, which gave him comfort.

"Sheriff, I know this is a lot to ask, but what card was found on your son?"

Sheriff Harper quickly turned his head over to look at Brenda, thinking of her question. Then he remembered the card his son was found with.

"It was the Jack of Clubs."

"Clubs? Did your son have any violent tendencies or aggression problems?"

"Yes, he had been in trouble for fighting when he was in high school before he went missing."

"And since his card was a Jack, he was chosen because the Keepers felt you had power in the community, I presume. I'm sure if you go back and look at all the other victims and the cards they were found with, you will be able to find out what was in their past that got them chosen." Brenda felt confident in her reasoning about the victims.

Sheriff Harper told Officer Colton to go back over the past victim's files and try to confirm Detective Wisely's observation. Officer Colton agreed to go back over the files because he wanted to be able to wrap his head around how something like this could have happened to all of those children. Officer Colton got up and left the Sheriff's office, leaving Brenda and the Sheriff alone to talk more.

Once they were alone, Brenda felt she had a plan to infiltrate the group; she just needed his permission to continue.

"Sheriff Harper, I have an idea about how I can find out who all is in the Keepers, but you may not like it," Detective Wisely prepared the Sheriff before telling him about her plan. "I want your permission to follow Samuel for a few days. I have a feeling that if he is involved with the Keepers, he will need to get in touch to warn them about our investigation."

"I agree and you have my full support, but if this gets too dangerous, you have to inform me as soon as possible so I can get some protection for you and your son. Do we have a deal?"

"Yes, sir, I appreciate your support, and I am confident I can do this without raising suspicion," Brenda told the Sheriff as she stood up and walked out of his office. She was prepared to begin her plan to infiltrate the group and discover who was leading the Keepers.

Before Brenda left the station, she stopped at the front desk to talk to Sophie.

"Sophie, can you get me Samuel Everest's home address and a list of vehicles registered in his name, please?"

"Of course, Detective Wisely. I will call you once I have the information you have requested."

"Thank you, Sophie. Also, will you keep this between us? I am just fascinated with how much information about Whispering Pines he knows. I don't want the other officers to make fun of me for being a history buff," Brenda asked Sophie, hoping she was trustworthy and not connected to the Keepers. Brenda was also unsure about what other officers she could trust with this information; the only officer she trusted was Officer Colton.

Brenda left the station and went straight to her car so she could drive by Samuel's office. She wanted to see if there were any vehicles parked in front of his office, since he said he had a meeting when he left her alone to look through the Keepers' box. She hoped she could get the license plate number of someone else who may be connected to the Keepers. As she drove by his office, the parking lot was empty, deflating her hopes of finding another connection to the Keepers.

Brenda had a feeling she would not have to follow Samuel long before he would attempt to contact the Keepers. She just had to be patient.

A few days had gone by with Brenda tailing Samuel's every move. She followed him to the grocery store, to his sister's house, the bank, and even to a doctor's appointment. Those few days were extremely boring for Brenda, but she never lost sight of her agenda. She just had to have more patience because she knew deep down inside herself, he would eventually break his pattern. She had to keep following him if she wanted to get to the truth about the Keepers.

The next day, Brenda noticed Samuel was driving out of Whispering Pines towards the country club. Brenda knew he was not a member of the club because of the annual membership cost and the monthly membership costs, which Samuel did not have. She had learned that Samuel led a modest life as a middle-class member of Whispering Pines after she investigated his finances. Though he was not poor, he was not financially stable enough to become a member of the country club. Add to that the fact that there were no records of any payments to the club in his finances. Brenda felt confident in her assumption.

Brenda could not follow behind Samuel as close as she would have liked, since Country Club Road was a long stretch of straight road with no places to hide. She allowed Samuel to drive ahead of her further than she liked, but it was necessary to keep her cover. There was a slight drop coming up in the road, right before the entrance to the country club, so as soon as Samuel's car was out of sight going down the hill, she sped up to get closer to him without being seen. She wanted to ensure she could clearly see Samuel turn off Country Club Road. By the time she made it up to the top of the hill, she could not see Samuel's car anywhere.

Brenda continued past the country club's entrance and did not see any sign of Samuel's vehicle on the property. This meant he had to have turned on another road down the hill, out of her sight. If he turned off Country Club Road when he was out of view from Brenda, she felt he might be on to her following him. Brenda was not going to let the idea of Samuel seeing her stop her from doing her job, so she pressed on.

Brenda made it to the end of Country Club Road, which ended at another highway. She looked both directions to see if she could see Samuel's car going either way but saw nothing. Not seeing Samuel's car on the highway, she decided to turn around and head back to Whispering Pines. On her way past the country club entrance, she noticed a dirt road after the club's entrance on the other side of the road. She could tell the road had just had a vehicle drive on it by the way the dust was filling the area, so she knew that was where Samuel had gone. She quickly turned her car onto the dirt road, knowing she was back on his trail. All Brenda had to do was follow the dust trail until it stopped; that's where she would learn if he had turned off the road. She was right. The dust trail stopped in front of a field with a cattle gate open to a vehicle path through the field.

Brenda decided to park her car away from the open cattle gate. This way, she could walk through the open field with the hopes of it leading to a place where the Keepers would meet. She exited her vehicle and began making her way down the vehicle path in the field. As she made her way through the field, the further she went, she began to notice a cabin at the end of the vehicle path. She made her way closer and closer to the cabin until she was able to confirm that Samuel's car was there, parked behind a few other vehicles. She knew then she was at the right place.

Once she made it to the cabin, she began to walk around it, looking into any window she could find to see if she could see where they were meeting. She was cautious as she peeked through each window, ducking down to avoid being detected by anyone inside the cabin. Brenda was making her way to another window further down from her location, but heard another car approaching the cabin, so she found an area where she could hide. She hoped to get a glimpse of who was joining the meeting, another suspect she could dig into. But when the vehicle parked, the occupants stepped out wearing black robes with hoods covering their faces. Seeing those people cemented her assumption that she was in the right place.

Brenda followed the two newcomers towards the back of the cabin, where they entered the cabin through a cellar door, one that did not actually lead into the cabin, but under it. She waited for them to enter the cellar and close the door before she made her way over to the doors leading to the cellar. Brenda sat there outside the cellar doors, giving the latecomers time to get to the bottom of the stairs leading down into the cellar. Even though she was not sure if there was a separate room in the cellar, she knew she had to breach the cellar. But before she was going to breach the doors, she wanted to take one more look around the cabin to see if there were any windows with a view of the cellar and not a view of the interior of the surface part of the cabin.

Brenda put her ear to the cellar doors but was unable to hear anything. This let her know she could enter the cellar without being seen.

After inspecting the exterior of the cabin, she knew that there were no windows for the cellar. She knew she had to take a chance on making an entry quickly. Since she was unable to hear anything through the cellar doors, she slowly lifted one of the doors, easing it open to make sure the door did not draw attention to herself. Seeing the door open with ease, she opened it up only enough for her to slide her body through a crack in the door. She slowly eased her way through the cracked cellar door and closed it just as slowly as she had opened it. Now that she was inside the cellar, she had to make some quick decisions, like finding a place to hide if anyone came towards the entrance and finding the actual room for the meeting of the Keepers.

Brenda began to scan the dark room of the entrance of the cellar, looking for a place to hide and a door to another room. She was able to quickly find a secure place to hide if someone came out of the meeting room, so she made her way over to the hiding spot. Once she felt she could not be seen from her location, she began to scan for another door in the room. After a few minutes in the dark, her eyes adjusted enough for her to see a door to another room. Finding a door that could lead to their meeting, she forced herself to move closer to it so she could try to hear what they were talking about. Brenda was scared she would be caught if she got too close to the door, but she knew she had no other choice. She quietly moved over to the door and pressed her ear up to it.

Brenda sat there for several minutes with her ear up to the door before she heard anything. She could hear people talking inside, but she could not hear them clearly. Not being able to hear them clearly, she decided to look for somewhere she might be able to see into the room. She felt that if she could not hear them, then if she could see some of them, she would be able to have other suspects to talk to in the hopes of turning them against the Keepers.

Moving around quietly in the cellar, she managed to find a small crack in the wall next to the door with a clear view of the room where the Keepers were. As she began to peer through the crack in the wall, she could hear them more clearly. As she spied on the Keepers during a secret meeting, she was able to identify several members of the group. One member she could identify was the one and only Ms. Carter, the school's secretary. The same Ms. Carter who was gathering information for Brenda about the Keepers, the group her parents supposedly talked about. Brenda knew right then Ms. Carter was trying to throw her off the Keepers' trail. Brenda's stomach began to tighten with the feeling of betrayal from Ms. Carter. Ms. Carter was one of the only people she felt she could trust in Whispering Pines. Ms. Carter's betrayal hurt Brenda deeply, and she was not going to let her get away with defying her in such a way.

As Brenda listened to the Keepers' meeting through the crack in the wall, she was unable to see the main person speaking, but she was able to identify the voice. She knew that voice, and it did not surprise her one bit to find that person was involved in the Keepers. Brenda was disgusted by what the voice was saying. How they had to continue the work of the Keepers of the Light if they wanted to ensure they all made it to heaven. They had to cleanse all of the families who had entrusted their own children with the Keepers to remove the shame from them by sacrificing their child to purify their souls.

Brenda felt she had heard and seen enough of the Keepers' meeting to be able to build a case against them for murder. She had to begin making her exit from the cellar, but before she could leave, someone started to open the door to the meeting room. Brenda reacted as quickly as possible to ensure she could get to her hiding spot before being found. She moved so quickly to her preselected hiding spot, fast enough to get there just as the door opened all the way.

As Brenda hid, her heart beating faster than ever from fear of being found by someone with the Keepers, she held her breath and tried to make sure she was hidden from anything that might walk out of the room. She remained still and silent in order not to be detected, as the people in the room began to exit it. As each member of the Keepers of the Light passed her location, Brenda's heart skipped a beat, thinking it could be any one of the members who would find her. She felt it was time to let the Sheriff know her location.

Brenda took out her phone from her pocket, holding it up to her chest to block the light from the screen, just long enough for her to turn down the brightness. Being satisfied that the light from her phone was low enough for her to send a text, that was exactly what she did. Brenda sent a short text to Sheriff Harper and Officer Colton with her location. The text read:

"Found Keepers. Hiding. May be in danger. If you don't hear from me in 15 minutes, this is my location."

With the text sent, Brenda began to relax a little, knowing the Sheriff and Officer Colton knew where she was and why she was there. She knew if anything happened to her, they would be able to find out who the culprit was. After sending the text, she put her phone back in her pocket on silent mode. She hid until each member of the Keepers walked past her in her hiding spot and exited the cellar. After the last member left the room, the door was closed behind them. Then there was the sound of a lock being attached to the door itself. Brenda's fear came right back to her in a flash. She knew then she was locked inside the cellar with no way out, but she did not let panic set in because she knew all she had to do was send another text to the Sheriff, and they would come to get her out of the cellar. She knew she had to wait before texting them again, because she needed to make sure all members were gone from the cabin before the Sheriff and Officer Colton showed up to blow her cover.

Fearing for her life, Brenda remained calm, knowing she would soon be rescued from her current situation alive thanks to the Sheriff and Officer Colton. She knew she had an out, but she knew she had to wait, because rushing anything at this time would only force the Keepers to go underground. She could not risk the Keepers separating and going underground, so he just took slow breaths, thinking about her son, Dalton.

Brenda held on to faith that she would get out of the cellar alive; she was not ready to leave her son alone in the world. She went through her memories of her and Dalton going on vacation and having such a good time, and of them moving to Whispering Pines. She was not ready to give up without a fight, so if any member of the Keepers came back down through the cellar doors, she was prepared to act. Brenda had her gun unholstered and aimed at the cellar entrance. She was taking no chances with someone coming back to finish her off. She knew if they found her car parked down the road from the field leading to the cabin, which was a possibility, they might come back to look for her.

Brenda sent another text before the fifteen minutes were up from her previous text to Sheriff Harper and Officer Colton. In her second text to them, she let them know she was okay but was locked in the cellar of the cabin at her location. She asked that they come to her location to assist her in getting out of the cabin's cellar. With the text sent, all Brenda had to do was wait for them to arrive, so that is what she did. She waited.

Chapter 10

The Final Confrontation

Brenda waited inside the cellar for another twenty minutes before Sheriff Harper and Officer Colton showed up to assist her with getting out of the locked cellar. As soon as she heard the lock on the outside of the cellar doors being cut, she felt relief. She knew if the lock was being cut and not unlocked with a key, it had to be the Sheriff or Officer Colton, not a Keeper member. Once the lock was cut and removed from the cellar doors, Officer Colton pulled the cellar doors open, letting light into the cellar. When Brenda looked up, she saw him standing at the top of the stairs with light all around him. The first thing that came to Brenda's mind was that Officer Colton was her savior.

Brenda stepped out of her hiding spot in the cellar and made her way towards the cellar doors, where Officer Colton was waiting for her. As soon as she made it to the top of the cellar doors, she gave Officer Colton a big hug and a quick thank you. Now that she was out of the cellar and safe, she told Officer Colton to take her up to her car and to follow her back to the station. She needed to brief both him and the Sheriff about what she had seen and heard.

Officer Colton did as he was instructed and took Brenda up to her car and followed her back to town to the Sheriff's station. He parked his car and made it into the station to meet with Detective Wisely and the Sheriff. He was anxiously waiting to hear what she found out during her time in the cellar. He continued into the station and down the hallway towards the Sheriff's office. As soon as he arrived at the Sheriff's office, he could see Detective Wisely already sitting in front of the desk, so he entered without knocking, following Detective Wisely's instructions. He walked in and took the empty chair beside the detective and waited for her to elaborate on what she found out.

After Officer Colton took his seat next to her, Brenda began to inform the Sheriff and Officer Colton of what she witnessed and heard during her time in the cellar of the cabin in the field where she had followed Samuel. She told them about seeing Ms. Carter, the school secretary, through the crack in the wall, and the voice she heard leading the meeting. She continued telling them about their true mission, how killing the children of the families who offered them to the Keepers would cleanse the family of all the sins committed by their child, or a child who could represent their own child. How they believed it was the only way for those families to secure a spot in heaven.

Hearing what Detective Wisely was telling them, neither of them could believe what she was saying. It was obvious to Brenda that they both were wondering how a group, such as the Keepers of the Light, could operate for so long right under their noses. She could tell they were beginning to beat themselves up in their heads for allowing such atrocities to happen in their town. So, Brenda felt she had to say something to bring them out of their own self-disbelief.

"Guys, this is not your fault. This group consists of individuals from nearly every business sector, including those from Whispering Pines and the surrounding counties. This group was in a position to cover their tracks by simply having members in the perfect positions to conceal their crimes. You have to know that and not blame yourselves. Now that we know more about them, we have the opportunity to do something. Which leads me to my next suggestion," Detective Wisely told the pair in the room.

Both Sheriff Harper and Officer Colton snapped out of their thoughts and agreed with Brenda. They knew they were now in a position to end the Keepers of the Light, and they were both ready to end the murderous religious zealots from ever being able to hurt or kill another helpless child. They both turned their attention over to Detective Wisely.

"What are you suggesting, Brenda?" Sheriff Harper asked her.

This was the first time Sheriff Harper had ever called her by her first name, which to her signified he acknowledged her as not just a coworker, but also as a friend. Brenda knew they were both ready to end the Keepers and all members of the group, regardless of who they were or the positions they held in any county.

"Thank you, Sheriff. Well, I think it's time to have a city council meeting, don't you?"

"I see where you are going with this, and I like it, detective. You want to call out the members within Whispering Pines in front of the residents of Whispering Pines. I think it will be interesting to see how they react to being called out in public. Not to mention, the families who had given their children to the Keepers. But how can we ensure they will all show up to the meeting?" Sheriff Harper asked Brenda.

"Easy, let the town think it is about raising property taxes here in Whispering Pines. From what I have learned in my years as a police officer here, that is the one thing that can pull everyone together to debate," Officer Colton quickly suggested to Sheriff Harper and Detective Wisely.

Brenda was impressed with how Officer Colton quickly came up with a solution to their current problem with getting everyone to attend a boring council meeting. She began to show a huge smile on her face, which Officer Colton noticed and began to smile back at her.

"You continue to amaze me, Officer Colton. That sounds like the perfect subject for a council meeting. It is definitely one that the people will want to attend, because no one wants their property taxes to increase. Just brilliant, Officer Colton, brilliant," Brenda expressed her appreciation towards Officer Colton, which comforted him.

Now that they had a plan in place to get the residents of Whispering Pines together in one place, all for the sole purpose of revealing the identity of a secret religious group of murderers in front of everyone, they continued to discuss when they would have this meeting. They wanted to make sure it was soon, to slow the Keepers down from killing another child, to fulfill a ridiculous way to earn a spot in heaven. They reviewed the plans for the council meeting and knew they needed someone from the Tax Appraiser's office to cooperate with them. That was when Brenda had a thought about who they could approach.

"Sheriff, I know who we can approach in the Tax Appraiser's Office, and I know they will help us. I can't tell you who just yet, but you have to trust me. He will do it," Brenda relayed to the Sheriff.

Sheriff Harper knew he could trust Brenda, so if she said she had someone who would help, he believed her.

"I trust you, Brenda, do what you have to do to get things rolling, but make it quick."

"Yes, sir. Thank you. I won't let either of you down," Brenda replied to the Sheriff before walking out of his office. She knew where she needed to go next, the Tax Appraiser's Office in Whispering Pines.

Brenda left the station, walked to her car, and once she was seated in her cruiser, she began making the drive over to the Tax Appraiser's Office down Main Street. The drive was short with no traffic, as there was never any traffic in Whispering Pines, unless a football game, a basketball game, or a rodeo parade was happening. Brenda pulled up and parked in front of the tax office, got out of her cruiser to make her way into the building. Upon entering the building, she was not surprised to be greeted by Christopher Wooden. She knew he had worked at the tax office building since he was terminated from the school as a teacher after being implicated in David Youngblood's murder. Even though he was found innocent of the murder, the school board felt that his being a suspect in Davie's murder was too much to allow him to continue teaching at the school. After being terminated from the school, Christopher was hired as a local Tax Assessor for Whispering Pines.

"Good afternoon, Detective Wisely. What brings you here today? I hope you are not here to investigate me about any of the current murders here in Whispering Pines," Christopher semi-jokingly said to Brenda.

"Hello, Christopher, no, I am not here to investigate you for anything. I was sorry to hear about your termination with the school because of the investigation into Davie's murder. I never intended to cause you any harm. I know how much you loved being a teacher." Detective Wisely offered a sincere apology to Christopher, who accepted.

"My separation from the school was not your fault. I should have said something much earlier about Davie's disappearance when it happened. So, what can I do for you now?"

"Thank you, Christopher. Since you asked, I do need a favor from you, or from the Tax Appraiser's Office to be exact."

"What can we do for you?"

"I'm glad you asked, Christopher. I need to see if your office can plan an emergency property tax increase meeting for Whispering Pines. I know it may sound strange, but it is just a way I can get everyone in Whispering Pines to show up to a council meeting at the same time. The topic of property tax increases is the easiest way to get everyone in the same place at the same time."

Christopher gave Detective Wisely a look of confusion. He felt that if Detective Wisely came to him to ask for a favor, it must be connected to a case she was working on, and he knew if he could help her in any way. He had to try.

"I won't even ask why you need the town together, and I will get together with my supervisor to see what we can do to get a meeting together as quickly as possible for you. Can you give us a couple of hours to see what we can come up with for you?"

"Of course, Christopher. I truly appreciate you doing this for me and not asking any questions. One more thing, I hope you can convince your supervisor that it needs to be kept between the three of us at all costs. It can't get out. I am the person requesting this fake meeting," Detective Wisely quickly expressed to Christopher how secrecy was of the utmost importance.

Christopher smiled at Detective Wisely and gave her a reassuring nod with his head.

With that, Brenda turned and walked away from Christopher to make her way back outside the tax office. Once again, she got back into her cruiser, but this time she was heading home for some lunch. Brenda made it home, went inside, and fixed herself some quick lunch. With her lunch ready, she sat down at the kitchen table and began eating. But before she could finish her lunch, she was interrupted by her phone ringing. She pulled her phone out of the breast pocket of her shirt and looked down, and saw it was from the tax office.

Brenda answered her phone as quickly as possible, "This is Detective Wisely."

"Hello, Detective Wisely, this is Christopher from the tax office. Do you have a moment to speak?"

"Of course, Christopher. Have you already been able to schedule something?"

"We have. How about a town meeting this Thursday? I know it's only two days away, but I had a feeling you would rather have the meeting sooner than later."

"Christopher, you are a miracle worker, and I will never forget what you have done for me today. Thank you so much, Christopher."

Brenda and Christopher discussed details such as what time the meeting would start and where they would hold it. They both agreed on having the meeting at the high school gym. Brenda chose the school gym because she knew she would be able to assign officers at the entrances and exits to keep people from leaving once the meeting started. She wanted to make sure the location would be a place the Sheriff's office could control, because once everyone from Whispering Pines was there, she could begin her real investigation of the Keepers of the Light.

After they had everything agreed as to location and time, Brenda gave Christopher the okay to get the flyers out to the public. She also suggested that he post something on their website. She would make sure Mark learned about the meeting so he could put a notice about it in tomorrow's newspaper. She wanted to ensure everyone knew about the property tax increase meeting on Thursday. They ended their call and began working on the provisions to ensure the meeting goes off without a hitch.

Brenda picked up the rest of her sandwich and grabbed some paper towels to wrap it in, and quickly left her home. She wanted to get to Mark's office so she could slip him some information he could post in the paper, something the people were not going to like: a town meeting about property taxes going up. She knew the people would object to the tax hike and would show up en masse.

Brenda jumped into her car and made her way to the town square so she could try to catch Mark at the office before it closed. She was extremely excited when she pulled up in front of his office door and noticed the lights were still on inside. She knew then Mark had not left for the day. Seeing he was still in his office, she jumped out of her car and quickly walked up to the office doors. As soon as she reached his front office doors, she pushed them open and made her way inside.

"Mark, are you in here?" Brenda spoke loudly as she entered the building.

Mark heard the door ding as Detective Wisely entered the building, and he headed toward the front door. He was in the back getting ready to start the printing press to get the paper ready for tomorrow's early deliveries, and before he could make it to the front, he heard Detective Wisely yelling his name.

"Hello, Detective Wisely, yes, I am here. I was in the back getting ready to put the paper to press. What can I do for you?"

"So, you have not printed the paper yet? Good, because I have something you may want to add to it."

"Really, what could be so important it couldn't wait until next week's paper?"

"Well, you didn't hear this from me, but I was over at the tax office earlier. I wanted to talk to someone about my property taxes from last year, and that was when I heard something I shouldn't have."

"Really? Do tell," Mark took the bait Brenda was giving him.

"Well, like I said, you didn't hear this from me, but you will find out tomorrow, and it will be too late for you to print it. That is why I am here. While I was at the tax office, I overheard two people in the back discussing their plans for a town meeting in two days about increasing property taxes for next year. But they didn't want to post it in the paper because the fewer residents who attended the meeting, the better chances they would have of getting it approved by the City Council. Now, as a resident here and a homeowner, there was no way I could let this get passed."

"Are you serious, Detective Wisely?"

"Please, call me Brenda. I am not here on a police matter, but as a resident of Whispering Pines, and yes, I am very serious. They are planning to post flyers tomorrow evening, just a few hours before the meeting. They figure that is the easiest way to give the town notice, and yet not have anyone attend. The meeting will be at the high school gym at 7:00 PM. I believed this needed to be announced earlier than they planned. Don't you agree?"

"I can't believe they are trying to increase our property taxes again. They have been trying to increase our property taxes for almost seven years, and every year it gets shut down by the town's folk, so this must be why they are doing it this way now. Thank you, Brenda, for informing me of this meeting. Now, I need to leave you so I can make a correction to the front page, print the paper, and try to get it out tonight, not tomorrow morning. I promise I will make sure you are not mentioned, since you can be my source," Mark assured Brenda that he would keep her out of the article and also make sure everyone knew about the meeting.

Brenda thanked Mark and left his office so he could make the necessary changes to the paper. She knew he had plenty of work to do for the night, which pleased her because she knew he wouldn't have time to do anything else around town.

Once she was outside, she got back into her car and made her way back over to the Sheriff's station. She wanted to update Officer Colton and Sheriff Harper on her progress in getting everyone together in only two days. She needed to get a plan together with the Sheriff about how they would get officers at the entrance doors and exit doors of the gym on Thursday, but only after the meeting started, once everyone was inside. She didn't want to inform the other officers about the meeting or their plan to draw out the Keepers of the Light because she was unsure whom she could trust at the Sheriff's office.

She parked her car in front of the station and quickly made her way into the station, past Sophie, and down the hallway to Sheriff Harper's office. She did not knock on his door but burst into his office instead. They had to get the plans together quickly since they only had two days.

She spent several hours in the Sheriff's office, planning with him and Office Colton, until they had a foolproof plan to make sure everyone was in place when they would be needed. Once they all felt confident in the plan, they concluded for the day.

***

Brenda woke up on Thursday with pins and needles running throughout her body. While she had confidence in their plan for the town meeting that evening, she was still unsure if her plan to draw out members of the Keepers of the Light would work. She knew it was too late to change her plan; she knew she had to go ahead and either draw the Keepers out or make them go underground. She felt she had a fifty-fifty chance of succeeding. To her, those odds felt better than most of her ideas in the past, so now she just had to wait for the meeting to start.

Brenda went out to the high school gym, double-checking her plan in her mind, thinking of anything that could go wrong that would change the outcome of the meeting. Brenda was very nervous that she would fail and never get the townspeople to believe what she was about to tell everyone at the meeting. Once she was sure she had gone over everything, the only thing left for her to do was wait.

Brenda spent the rest of the day waiting, trying not to think about the outcome of her attempt to draw out a zealot group called the Keepers of the Light, who used the murders of children as a way for families of the group to secure a place in heaven. She knew she was going to try to draw out members of the Keepers from

Whispering Pines, but she also knew the group was much larger than just Whispering Pines. Her only hope was that if she could pull this off, she could persuade the local members of the group to reveal the other members from the counties surrounding Whispering Pines. She hoped she would be able to shut the Keepers down for good; she wanted to make sure no more children would be killed for a foolish notion of being able to secure a spot in heaven by committing murder, especially the murder of children with some possible issues.

The time had come for the town meeting about property tax increases, and as she waited outside the high school gym, she was not surprised to see how many residents of Whispering Pines showed up for it. She knew the only reason so many residents were present at the meeting was because of the article Mark put on the front page of the Whispering Pines Gazette.

Brenda was not surprised to see the Whispering Pines Gazette that morning and the front-page article about how the tax assessors were trying to raise our property taxes this year without us being able to fight it by their nasty tactics of posting late flyers only hours before the meeting and how he had a source who informed him of their intentions two days before they planned their meeting. Mark went all out trying to make the tax officers look so corrupt that the people of

Whispering Pines would have no option but to attend the meeting.

People were arriving at the school gym, discussing how the tax office, trying to increase property taxes behind their backs, was wrong and how they had to come up with a way to end the corruption in Whispering Pines' offices. Brenda sat in her car until she felt it was time for her to enter the gym as a concerned resident wanting to try to keep her property taxes from increasing. She needed people to see her coming into the building just as upset as they were; she needed them to accept her as one of them, if only in the beginning.

Brenda entered the gym, took a seat in the back, and began making small talk with Emily, her neighbor and friend, about how something like this could happen in a small town. The talking amongst the groups continued until the Sheriff felt the majority of the residents were present. Once he was sure, he looked over at Christopher, letting him know it was time to start the meeting.

Christopher walked up to the podium that was placed on the stage in the gym for the town meeting. But before he began to speak, he quickly asked Detective Wisely to join him on stage.

Brenda took her cue from Christopher, stood up, and began walking up to the stage. Once she was standing next to Christopher, she stepped in front of the microphone. She thanked Christopher for getting the meeting together so quickly at her request. This caused the residents of Whispering Pines to look at each other in confusion. People started talking among themselves, asking if anyone knew what was going on, but of course, no one knew except Brenda, Sheriff Harper, and Officer Colton. Brenda quickly wanted to stop the talking in the crowd so she could explain why she had called them all there that day.

"Hello neighbors, if you could please stop talking, I would be happy to explain what is going on here tonight," Brenda spoke to the town people on the microphone.

The residents of Whispering Pines all stopped talking just as quickly as they started, once Brenda asked them to. They all wanted to know what was going on and why they were all there.

Once the crowd was quiet, Brenda spoke into the microphone again. "Thank you. Now that I have your attention, please allow me to explain why I have created this ruse with the help of the Tax Assessor's Office. Just to make it clear, this is not a meeting about our property taxes being increased or any wrongdoing by the officers of the Tax Assessor's Office; this is actually because we, at the Sheriff's office, want you all to know about something that has been going on here in Whispering Pines for over forty years. This is hard for me to tell you, but there has been a religious group, or more zealots, who have been murdering children from Whispering Pines, thinking it was the only way for families of this group to secure a place in heaven. I know this may sound absurd to you, but I can tell you it is all true." Brenda began telling the people of the town she loved so much about how such horrific events have been happening without their knowledge.

"Now, as I look around the room, I can assure you there are at least three members of the group here with us tonight. You may be asking yourselves how I know for sure that three members are here. Well, that's easy. You see, I was able to follow one of the members to a secret meeting the other day. It was held down FM 149, the dirt road just before the County Club entrance on the left side of Country Club Road. I followed said member down FM 149 until I noticed his car had turned into a field through an open cattle gate. I parked my car a little further away from the open cattle gate, then walked back to the entrance and through the field until I reached a cabin at the end of the trail. Upon reaching the cabin, I was able to make my way inside and hid in the basement of the cabin. Once I was inside the basement, I found a crack in a wall through which the meeting was going on the other side. I sat and listened. While looking inside, I was able to identify one person because I saw them, and I recognized another by their voice. I again was able to verify their identity when they walked past me while I was in a hiding spot, after their meeting.

Now, the things I heard during that meeting, coming from the voice I know, were horrific. They spoke about murdering more children to make sure members of the group were going to go to heaven when they died. I was sickened by his words.

Since I have your attention, let me provide you with a little more information. The group is called the Keepers of the Light, and the three members I know for sure are here are Ms. Carter, the secretary from Whispering Pines High School, Mr. Samuel Everest, the local historian, and finally, the leader of the group is our one and only local journalist and owner of Whispering Pines Gazette. Now, before you try to take off, the exits are all covered, and you will not be allowed to leave." Brenda stopped speaking and watched everyone in the audience looking around, trying to find the three she had just called out.

Brenda was pleased with how the crowd was reacting after hearing about the Keepers. She had a feeling Ms. Carter, Mr. Everest, and Mark were probably the only members of the Keepers present during the meeting. She decided to allow the audience to speak out loud and voice the shame they felt towards the members of the Keepers who had been called out. She also enjoyed how the three of them were trying to get together to make a quick exit, but the town was not going to allow that. The night went on for a few more hours before the officers grabbed the three of them to take them to the station and place them under arrest.

Chapter 11

Healing Wounds

Once Sheriff Harper, Officer Colton, and Brenda had Ms. Carter, Mr. Samuel Everest, and Mark Thompson in custody and removed from the school gym, it was time for Brenda to explain to the remaining residents of Whispering Pines what had just happened. She had already filled in Mayor Laura Jenkins about what was going to happen at the town meeting and knew she would need the mayor's help in reassuring the residents that they were in no danger. She decided to allow Mayor Jenkins to address the town's fold.

"Can I get your attention, please? I want to address you tonight, not only as the mayor of Whispering Pines, but also as a concerned parent." Mayor Jenkins openly spoke to the residents.

Mayor Jenkins' soft-spoken voice brought the unsettled residents into silence. Everyone stopped talking amongst themselves long enough for them to compose themselves and take their seats. Once all eyes were on Mayor Jenkins, she was ready to begin informing them of the current situation in Whispering Pines.

"Thank you all for being here tonight. I know what has transpired here today was not only confusing but also shocking for everyone to witness. Detective

Wisely and the sheriff's office have been investigating a zealot group responsible for murdering an unknown number of children over the past forty years. We do know for sure that at least four of the children were from Whispering Pines. One of the first victims from Whispering Pines was the daughter of a local Reverend who worked at the old church that closed down several years ago. It is believed that the Reverend gave his daughter over to the Keepers of the Light, which was apparently a place where wayward children could go to be reacquainted with the teachings of the Bible. It was for children who sinned daily. While the children believed they were put there to be helped, the parents and the group leaders knew the children were there to be sacrificed for their family to secure a place in heaven." Mayor Jenkins began revealing more details about the children who were murdered and why they were murdered.

The audience was still silent, but she could see the disgust on their faces. Mayor Jenkins knew they were having the same feelings and thoughts as she did. How could our faith be so misconstrued in such a horrible way? She knew what she had to do next.

"I know how you all are feeling at this moment, but we still need your help if we want to ensure the Keepers of the Light are shut down for good. I implore everyone here tonight to think about this group. We need everyone to think about what I have just told you. I encourage you to contact the sheriff's office if you think you have any information about the group or who else could be a member. We can also confirm that this group has members in very high places, not only in Whispering Pines leadership, but also in the surrounding counties. Their members could be anyone from here or around us, so think hard and contact the sheriff's office. We want to be able to shut the entire group down, not just the members from Whispering Pines. I hope we can count on your help in this horrific zealot group of religious extremists," Mayor Jenkins concluded the evening meeting.

The residents of Whispering Pines had their instructions, and while the majority of them had no information to relay to the sheriff's office, there was a small group who thought they might have something to tell the officers. The audience dispersed from the school gym, and the sheriff's officers ended the majority of their shifts for the day once the gym was cleared. Those officers scheduled for the night shift made their way back to the station to get their assignments for the night.

Back at the station, Brenda, Officer Colton, and Sheriff Harper each had one of the known members of the Keepers of the Light in an interrogation room, trying to break them enough to reveal any other unknown members of the group who reside in Whispering Pines.

Brenda chose to interrogate Ms. Carter. She was convinced that Ms. Cater knew more about the group's members than just being a member. She already knew Ms. Carter knew about Reverend Johnson and the Keepers of the Light. Since Brenda had witnessed her at the secret meeting in the cabin, she knew she could fill in a lot of blanks in her investigation into the group. She had to know who founded the group and who the head leaders were.

It was not hard for Brenda to break Ms. Carter during the interrogation. Brenda was surprised to learn about the high positions the leaders of the Keepers of the Light held in the surrounding counties; she was appalled. Brenda grasped that many of the leaders of the Keepers held positions such as sheriff, mayor, school principals, council members, bank presidents, and many other prominent political positions. She could not believe how far the Keepers had spread into all the surrounding counties. Brenda knew if they could dig deep enough into the Keepers, they could shut down one of the largest murder rings in local history. While Brenda knew she would be able to identify the local members and prosecute them, she also knew the other members would have to be investigated and tried by their respective counties due to their current positions within their counties. Brenda did release the information she had uncovered during her own investigation within the Keepers of the Light to the people of the counties, not presumed to be members of the group.

***

After four months of continuous investigating, Brenda, Officer Colton, and Sheriff Harper were able to identify Ms. Carter, Mark Thompson, and Samuel Everest as the only current local members of the Keepers in Whispering Pines. Brenda felt a sense of relief knowing only three members of the Keepers were from Whispering Pines, but while the number in her town was low, the number in their surrounding countries was much higher.

D.A. Parker was able to successfully prosecute the three local members of the Keepers with several counts of capital murder, child endangerment, child abuse, child neglect, and many other charges, enough charges to get them all life in prison with no possibility of parole. With the conviction of the Whispering Pines Three, the other counties would be able to convict their members of the Keepers with either the same crimes or similar charges. Brenda knew it would take years before the Keepers were completely shut down and dismantled but knowing it would happen one day was all she and the residents of Whispering Pines needed before they could begin to heal as a community.

After the convictions of Ms. Katherine Carter, Mr. Samuel Everest, and Mark Thompson, the current owner of the Whispering Pines Gazette, Mayor Jenkins felt it was time for her to have another town meeting. One where she could address the town about her feelings and thoughts on the corruption discovered within their community. Mayor Jenkins is a town leader who balances politics with community well-being, ensuring the town's prosperity and safety while navigating the fallout from the investigation of the Keepers in Whispering Pines. She needed to address them and reassure them of her continuous faith in Whispering Pines residents and how they can make peace with the horrific crimes the Keepers committed within their town.

Mayor Jenkins scheduled a mandatory meeting for the residents of Whispering Pines, as well as the smaller towns in the county, to address her position on the subject. The meeting was scheduled one week after the last of the Whispering Pines Three was sentenced. She wanted to make sure each of the local members involved with the Keepers was properly sentenced before making any public statement about the group.

With the announcement of Mayor Jenkins' town meeting, the residents of Whispering Pines felt it would be a great time to gather together once again as a community to show their support to do whatever was needed to heal as a community. They needed to try to bring peace to the families of the children who were picked by the Keepers to fulfill another member's request to secure a place in heaven, even if their own children were not sinners or if they had no children to sacrifice. All the child victims were innocent victims who had no way to protect themselves from a perverse religious zealot group that didn't want to help them, but only to murder them in the Lord's name for nothing more than their own delusional beliefs on how to make sure people can go to heaven.

The day had come for the town meeting with Mayor Jenkins, and the town was ready. People showed up on the city square with anticipation of hearing what Mayor Jenkins was going to say. Everyone loved Mayor Jenkins because of her commitment to the town as a descendant of one of the founders of Whispering Pines. Not only was she committed to Whispering Pines, but her entire family had been there for the community. Without their support and appreciation of her entire family tree, Whispering Pines would not have survived and grown as much as it had over the centuries. The town's folk respected her as well as her words.

Mayor Jenkins took the center of the gazebo in the middle of the town square, ready to address her people, the residents of Whispering Pines. She was so pleased to see just how many residents showed up, one in particular, June Youngblood. Everyone in town knew how Detective Wisely was able to solve the cold case of Davie Youngblood, bringing peace to his mother, June. Seeing June in the audience gave Mayor Jenkins the strength to speak to everyone in town. After seeing June, Mayor Jenkins began to tap the top of the microphone, making a small noise to get the attention of her audience, which worked very well. The town's folk quickly settled down and started to give Mayor Jenkins their full attention.

"Hello, Whispering Pines! It's good to see you were all able to make it here tonight. I appreciate you all being here tonight to discuss the horrific events that have been uncovered here in Whispering Pines. Before I begin tonight, I want to give a special welcome to June Youngblood. She is here tonight among you all, after healing from her own tragic events that happened in her life. I want to express how sorry we all are as a community for the loss of your amazing son, David, 'Davie' Youngblood, and I personally want to thank you for being here tonight with us. You are proof that we can survive such terrible acts within the community, as you have been able to find peace from your loss. You are truly an inspiration to us all, so again, thank you for being here tonight," Mayor Jenkins proceeded before beginning to speak about her true intentions for the night's meeting.

"Now that I have your undivided attention, I want to start out tonight's meeting with a big 'Thank you' to everyone in Whispering Pines. Detective Wisely's investigation brought light to a group of people who committed despicable crimes against not only the children of Whispering Pines, but also the children of all the other counties surrounding us here. What is more upsetting to learn about the group is the fact that they not only selected children based on cards drawn from a deck to determine what type of child would be murdered that year, but also the fact they murdered a young mother of Whispering Pines, kept her child until he was almost eighteen, then murdered him because of the fact he was conceived out of wedlock. It's appalling to hear that such atrocities happened here, in our town, under our own noses. I am not here to reflect back on what happened, but more on what we can do as a community to make sure something like this never happens again. We have to be more observant within our own community, being able to recognize when something is happening that may be wrong, and the strength to be able to make such things known to the Sheriff's Office. We are all here to watch out for each other and support each other, so eliminating violent crimes within our town should also be something we are all committed to achieving here," Mayor Jenkins expressed in her opening comments of the meeting.

The people of Whispering Pines knew Mayor Jenkins was sincere in her remarks because they all knew of her family's past and her current commitments to the town. Major Jenkins was not going to allow one group to devalue the love and support the residents of Whispering Pines had for each other and the town. She was committed to the growth of the town and of the people. She wanted the residents to be reassured she was not about to let the Keepers destroy everything they had all sacrificed to ensure Whispering Pines would prosper as one of the greatest communities and counties in the great state of Texas.

Once Mayor Jenkins was finished with her address to the residents of Whispering Pines, she knew they all felt the same way she did, and they would continue to be respectable and trusting residents of their town. At the end of the meeting, she knew she had the support of everyone in attendance. That feeling gave Mayor Jenkins the energy she needed to continue her work as the mayor of Whispering Pines.

Brenda was present during the town's meeting on the square with Mayor Jenkins addressing the residents and was pleased to hear everything Mayor Jenkins said. She was even more pleased to hear Mayor Jenkins recognize June Youngblood in the audience and thanked her for being there tonight, acknowledging the emotion and physical turmoil she had been through with the loss of her son, Davie Youngblood, the cold case she had solved. Brenda knew Mayor Jenkins meant every word she said during tonight's meeting. Brenda respected the mayor more than ever after the night's meeting. Brenda felt the town would be able to move forward from the town's recent horrific events.

Robert Starnes

Chapter 12

Moving Forward

Mayor Jenkins instilled a sense of prosperity within the community at her town meeting. The residents of Whispering Pines left the town meeting with a sense of self-worth with Mayor Jenkins. They all knew she would never do anything to cover up a crime and would do everything in her power to lead the town's people towards knowledge their town was safe. Mayor Jenkins promised her constituents she would do anything for Whispering Pines to ensure the people of the town would always come first. The people knew she meant it and they also knew she would bring justice to the parents of the victims who lost their lives at the hands of the Keepers of the Light.

***

After several months, all of the members of the Keepers of the Light were arrested and charged with the same charges as the Whispering Pines Three and convicted of said charges. The people of Whispering Pines had been able to put aside their fears and pray for the families of all the victims, even those families who offered their own child to the group. The town's folk felt those parents were the ones who needed the most prayers, because they committed an unforgivable sin.

With the town moving on with help from Mayor Jenkins, Brenda's workload had become just lighter over the past few months. With all the extra time on her hands, Brenda and Dalton made weekly visits out to see June, Davie's mother. They both enjoyed their time out visiting June. Dalton made sure all her yard work was taken care of, while Brenda made sure June continued healing from the loss of her son. Brenda and Dalton built a strong bond with June over the past year, and they knew June would be a part of their lives forever moving forward. Their bond with June was not the only bond they began making in Whispering Pines.

While Dalton was able to continue bonding with the other kids at school, Brenda and Emily's friendship grew. Anytime Dalton was out with his friends, and if Brenda had a free night, she would always reach out to Emily first. Emily would take Brenda out to meet other women of the town for a night of either teaching each other how to cook different meals, or just having a wine down Wednesday. The ladies would talk about the men of town some nights, then on other nights they would swap good books to read, but to them, it was not a book club. None of the women of Whispering Pines would ever be a part of a book club, they felt that was for women from big cities, not small towns.

Silence in Whispering Pines

It had only been a year and a half since she picked up and moved her and her son, Dalton, to Whispering Pines, but the longer they were there, the more she felt she made the right decision moving there. Since Brenda and Dalton moved to Whispering Pines, she had already solved a ten-year-old code case, giving closure to one of her now closest friends, June. Brenda had also cleared up a child murdering group, the Keepers of the Light, with the help of Sheriff Harper and Officer Colton. If not for Sheriff Harper's relentlessness for wanting closure for the murder of his own son, Brenda would never have been able to solve the mystery.

Dalton also had an amazing year and a half, because he was halfway through his junior year and his grades were at their highest. He was on the road to becoming Valedictorian of his junior class, president of their student council, quarterback for their varsity football team, and president of their debate club. Dalton was not dating anyone, as he was completely focused on his schoolwork by also taking college courses with a focus on an associate degree in forensics so he could continue on for a bachelor's degree from the only college near Whispering Pines, which was in the closest town near Whispering Pines. He wanted to stay close to the place he called home, and to be close to this mother.

Sheriff Harper was re-elected as the sheriff of Whispering Pines because of his help with the Keepers of the Light cases. The town's folk felt as long as Sheriff Harper was in charge of the officers hired to ensure their safety, they would be safe. Sheriff Harper was able to finally release his guilt for now begin able to solve, or prevent, his son's murder years before. Knowing his son was going to be able to rest in peace, Sheriff Harper quit drinking and began eating healthy. He wanted to ensure he would be willing and able to do whatever was necessary in order to keep Whispering Pines safe from ever having to be blindsided by another hateful group, or anyone who wanted to harm his citizens.

Officer Colton was promoted to detective and was assigned to assist Detective Wisely for his work in the Keepers cases. He and his wife were happy to hear Brenda accepted their offer of becoming their unborn child's godmother, which Brenda felt she could never refuse their offer, because to her and Dalton, Michael Colton and his wife Patricia was already a part of their family, ever since he was able to get her out of the Keepers secret cabin alive.

The people of Whispering Pines never spoke about the Whispering Pines Three, Ms. Carter, Mr. Everest, and Mr. Thompson, after they were charged and convicted for the parts they played within the Keepers of the Light. The town felt in order to be able to move forward, they needed to put the past behind them, especially by never speaking about them ever again. The Whispering Pines Three put a stain on the town, but with the help of Mayor Jenkins, the stain was removed. The town was flourishing with several new small businesses, along with a new owner of the Whispering Pines Gazette.

One day on Brenda and Dalton's visits with June, while Dalton was cleaning away some down tree branches lining the back end of June's property, next to a creek, Dalton began to smell something he could only describe as death. At first, Dalton thought it could possibly be a dead animal in the creek, so he paid no attention to it. Dalton continued to clear the dead tree branches until the back of June's property was free from possible fire hazards. With the clearing completed, Dalton made his way back into June's home where a big glass of sweet tea was waiting for him. He didn't feel it was necessary to mention the smell of a dead animal to his mother, so when she asked how everything went, he simply said, "All clear." Dalton picked up the glass of sweet tea and drank it in one large gulp. Clearing those tree branches was not only hard work, but also dehydrating work as well.

Brenda and Dalton finished up their visit with June and began their way home. Dalton was ready to take a shower after clearing June's dead tree branches from her property and wash the day off of him. As they drove home, Dalton let it slip he smelled something so bad coming from the creek behind June's property. He told her he thought it was more than likely a dead animal and was nothing to worry about, Brenda did not agree with her son.

"Dalton, did you go down into the creek and verify it was a dead animal?"

"Of course not, mom, but do you think there could be a dead body behind June's property, or could it be simply a dead animal? It's not like June lives in town, but out here in the sticks. A simple deduction of what could be possible out there would lead towards the smell being from a dead animal, not a person," Dalton quickly responded to his mother.

"While you may think the power of deduction is the only tool, we use in solving crimes, it is not. The quickest way to determine if the smell is coming from a dead animal, or a human being, is to make a visual confirmation, meaning going down into the creek and finding the source of the smell. Now, since you did not go into the creek to verify the source of the smell, we will need to go back," Brenda quickly schooled her son on the art of determining how to confirm if a crime was committed.

Dalton put his head down, knowing his mother was right, feeling foolish for not going into the creek to get visual confirmation it was an animal.

Brenda noticed the defeat her son was feeling by witnessing her son's subtle head bend and wanted to clear something up with him.

"Dalton, I am not telling you this to make you feel bad, I am giving you information you won't find in a schoolbook. Not only do you have to rely on your gut feelings, but you also must have to trust but verify. Your gut can play tricks on you at times, so, the only way to confirm if your gut was right or not is to go and make a simple visual inspection of the area. You look for the source, so in the future you can learn when to trust your gut and when not to," Brenda explained to her son, who seemed to perk up a bit.

Brenda had already turned her car around and began going back to June's. She wanted to go back to June's in order for her and her son to go down into the creek to find the source of the smell. Brenda was not trying to prove her son wrong, but she wanted to instill a sense of responsibility in order for him to succeed in a life of solving crimes.

As Brenda approached June's home, she parked closer to the creek on the back of June's property, trying to not be near June's home because she did not want to worry June in any way. Brenda quickly parked her car next to the short bridge that crossed the creek behind June's property. After parking, she asked Dalton to get out of the car and follow her down the creek with some flashlights she had in the trunk of her car. Now, with flashlights in their hands, she leads Dalton down the side of the bridge leading their way to the creek bed. Once she is sure they are on the creek bed, she continues walking towards June's property, where her land and the creek meet. The closer they got, the more she smelled the same smell he assumed her son smelled while clearing the dead tree branches from June's land near the creek.

While the smell was something Brenda had smelled too many times before than she could count, she began to brace herself because she felt she was about to find a dead body, and she needed to be prepared with what she was going to tell Dalton. She was overwhelmed with the fear of introducing her own son into the world of curt people could inflict on another person. As they approached the source of the smell, Brenda stopped quickly, then looked back at her son.

"Mom, why did you stop? It is a dead body?" Dalton quickly asked his mother.

Brenda took a moment before answering her son's question but then quickly prepared him for what they were about to see.

"Dalton, can you come a little closer, please? I need to show you something you may not want to see."

Dalton did as his mother asked and made his way up to her side. He was prepared for what he was afraid he was about to see. The closer he got to his mother's side Dalton began to notice something he thought he knew all along. It was a dead deer.

"I told you mom the smell was coming from a dead animal, not a person," Dalton reassured his mother he knew the origin of the smell was from an animal, not a person.

Brenda was relieved to find a dead deer instead of a dead body, not only for her and her son's sake, but also for June's sake. Now, with confirmation there was no dead body behind June's home, Brenda instructed Dalton to help her remove the remains of the deer from the creek, because she did not want June to have to smell the decay of the deer from her house. Dalton agreed with his mother and helped her remove the remains and take them to the other side of the creek.

Once the deer's remains were away from June's property, Brenda asked her son to go and retrieve a shovel from the trunk of her car so they could properly bury it, so the smell would not linger onto June's property. When they finished burying the deer remains, they went back up to the car so they could make their way back home. Dalton quickly understood what his mother was telling him about feeling one thing but knowing something are two totally different instincts. Dalton knew from then on, he had something to work on that was not taught in a book, but more from people with hands-on experience. The rest of their ride home was done in silence, because Brenda did not want to make her son feel incompetent but wanted him to know there is always more to the job than just feeling something.

About the Author

Robert Starnes was born in a small town in Northeast Texas, where his journey with the written word began. In middle school, he discovered a love for writing short stories, a passion that blossomed despite the challenges he faced with dyslexia. To overcome his learning disability, Robert immersed himself in reading books that were adapted into movies, exploring the differences between the written and visual narratives. This practice not only improved his understanding of language but also enriched his appreciation for storytelling.

With a professional background in customer service and property management that spans over 24 years, Robert's experiences bring depth and authenticity to his writing. His diverse career has given him a keen insight into human nature, which is reflected in his characters and storylines.

Robert's first published work was *The Multifamily Housing Guide – Leasing 101* in 2016, a guide aimed at assisting new leasing professionals in the multifamily housing industry. His guide provided practical tools and advice to help them succeed in their new career, making their transition easier and more efficient.

Building on his early success, Robert ventured into the world of fiction, writing the *Saving History Series,* a young adult historical fiction series. The five-book series has earned him the title of #1 best seller on Amazon, and the second book of the series debuted at #64 on Barnes & Noble's top 100. His novels draw inspiration from the past, present, and future, offering readers captivating and thought-provoking narratives.

Robert broke out into Science Fiction when he wrote A.N.D.R.E. (Advanced Neural-Based Digital Reasoning Entity) (Sept. 2024), a novel about the rise and fall of Artificial Intelligence in the future. While humans were forced to move underground the surface of the Earth to live, A.I.B.s (Artificial Intelligence Being) reigned over the surface for decades, until one of the first A.I.B.s, Andre made his way to a human colony with a plan to end the A.I.B.s rule over the surface.

John Grisham is one of Robert's favorite authors, though he also finds inspiration in the works of Suzanne Collins, Stephenie Meyer, Dan Brown, and Jobie Hughes. In his spare time, Robert enjoys baking cakes, reading, and working in property management.

Robert Starnes continues to captivate readers with his storytelling, blending his unique perspective and experiences into each work. Be sure to watch for his upcoming books and projects!

Books by Robert Starnes

Saving History Series

Time Keeper (2018)

School Bound (2019)

Search Begins (2019)

Loose Ends (2019)

Final Hour (2021)

Whispering Pines Mysteries

Echoes in Whispering Pines (2025)

The Multifamily Housing Guide Series

Leasing 101: Garden Style (2018)

Assistant Manager 101 (2023)

Books Published by Starnes Books LLC

Novel Study – Time Keeper – Patricia Carpenter (2018)

Trip of a Lifetime – Eric K. Reinholt (2020)

Moving On From Life's Challenges – Mindy Briggs (2022)

Editing completed by

Carpenter Editing Services, Inc.

Silence in Whispering Pines

www.ingramcontent.com/pod-product-compliance
Lightning Source LLC
Chambersburg PA
CBHW030141010826
48973CB00002B/674